THINGS THAT GO BUMP IN THE NIGHT

PATRICK CARMAN

THINGS THAT GO BUMP IN THE NIGHT

SCHOLASTIC PRESS/NEW YORK

PC STUDIO

Copyright © 2011 by PC Studio, Inc.

All rights reserved. Published by Scholastic Press, an imprint of Scholastic Inc., *Publishers since 1920.* SCHOLASTIC, SCHOLASTIC PRESS, and associated logos are trademarks and/or registered trademarks of Scholastic Inc.

Library of Congress Cataloging-in-Publication Data Available

ISBN 978-0-545-38475-9

10 9 8 7 6 5 4 3 2 1   11 12 13 14 15
Printed in the U.S.A.   23
First edition, September 2011

The text type was set in Georgia.
Book design by Christopher Stengel
Design elements by Joshua Pease

For Edgar
R.I.P.

CONTENTS

3:15 means several things. It's a time when things go bump in the night. A place where spooky stories find a home. A feeling . . . that chill running down your spine. 3 stands for listen, read, and watch, because that's what you do with a 3:15 story. 15 is for how long it's going to take you, 15 minutes or less.

My name is Paul Chandler, and I'll introduce you to each story. If you're brave enough to continue, you'll read for about ten minutes. Read the words and you'll have unlocked the ending: a video that will show you how the story ends.

I advise leaving the lights on.

Step inside, it's 3:15.

Paul Chandler

Visit www.315stories.com if you'd like to see the forest and hear my voice. I'll be waiting.

FOR AN AUDIO INTRODUCTION TO THIS
STORY, VISIT WWW.315STORIES.COM

PASSWORD: CODY

Clarence Buchanan was born in the small town of Marshall, Wisconsin, all the way back when it was known as Bird's Ruin, which is to say a very long time ago. So long ago, in fact, that people around Marshall were amazed Clarence was still alive in the late autumn of 1941. It was a simpler time for a man of ninety-one to finally meet his maker.

They say Clarence was born of fire, and that's true enough. As a younger man, he talked sometimes about the blaze that tore through Bird's Ruin the year he was born, how it gutted the tiny settlement and scattered most of those who survived to the wind. But Clarence had a willful, arrogant father, a man of the woods who was good with an ax and a shotgun. Marshall Buchanan kept his family on, taught young Clarence to fell the tallest trees and gun down rabbits, deer, moose, and bear — anything with four legs that moved and didn't bark or purr at the side of his leg.

The town grew again and Marshall Buchanan, who loved his ax more than any other tool he owned, tried to change the name from Bird's Ruin to Hatchetville, which seemed to him a very manly name for a town. But to Marshall's bitter disappointment, Asahel Hanchett, an upstart business tycoon, tricked the mayor into something close to Hatchetville, but not quite.

*Hanchett*ville.

After that, Marshall and his son moved out into the forest for good and entered Hanchettville only to trade chopped wood for supplies. It was about five years later when the accident occurred.

Clarence should have known better. He should have been more careful. He shouldn't have been anywhere near the clearing to begin with. But he was so excited he just ran and ran until he could hear his father's ax hitting a tree. They'd voted to change the name of the town once more, and Clarence carried the news.

Marshall, Wisconsin. Just like Marshall Buchanan.

How sad that Marshall was also the name of a real estate broker who had purchased most of Hanchettville's assets and had renamed the town after himself.

This was a fact that eluded young Clarence as he ran through the woods with the grand news that the town had finally honored Marshall Buchanan as a founding father.

Clarence ran down the narrow valley just as a 150-foot tree came crashing toward the ground. He was fifteen years old and fast, but not fast enough. His hand, the very hand he'd waved with a piece of paper that told of the good news, lay crushed between a boulder and the gigantic fallen tree. Marshall Buchanan's massive ax blade lay buried in the trunk as the boy's scream filled the fog-covered wood.

No one saw Clarence or his dad for a long time after that. In fact, no one ever saw Marshall Buchanan again. Only Clarence appeared now and then with two horses and a rusted-out trailer full of wood he traded for flour and sugar and oil. And he never let anyone help him unload the cargo of fallen, cut trees. He did it by himself, hurling the sharp metal hook of his left hand into the heavy wood and putting his whole body into the effort. He was a huge man by then, bearded and tall and 250 pounds of woodsman. His small dark eyes watched the world and he nearly never spoke. The hook did the talking for him, or so it seemed, as he pointed it to a bag of rice or a pot of grease at the general store.

And then one day the hook on Clarence Buchanan's hand changed. It is said that it happened after his father's death, that Clarence melted the family fortune on the cast-iron stove inside the hut in which they lived, that he fashioned an iron mold and poured the gold inside. That he made the golden hook and wore his treasure on his sleeve from that day forward.

For a time, people saw the hook and wondered about it, whispering when it passed by. The big man with the golden hook, lumbering through town with his burlap bag of provisions thrown over one great shoulder, was a mystery no one fully understood. They could not have guessed how much the hook was worth, because Clarence wore sleeves all the time and only the hook itself was ever seen by a living soul.

Still, for a time the golden hook gained quite a lot of notoriety.

Years passed and Clarence grew ever more mysterious, visiting town less frequently, until one day he stopped coming into town altogether.

And so it was that many years later, when Clarence Buchanan was approaching his death, the golden hook had become more legend than fact. It had been largely forgotten in the preceding twenty years as Clarence became more and more of a hermit. Toward the end, very few people ever saw Clarence or the hook.

At ninety-one and alone in the woods, there was but one person who'd seen him much lately, and that was Cody Miller, who we turn our attention to now.

Cody Miller, a down-on-his-luck seventeen-year-old, had the unenviable task of delivering groceries to all the shut-ins around town. It had fallen to him in recent months to trudge all the way out into the woods and bring Clarence Buchanan what he needed on Friday afternoons. Whoever had done it before Cody had left town altogether, and the golden hook had drifted further still into legend.

There was a short but meaningful conversation the first time Cody met Clarence Buchanan in the woods, which began like this:

"Me and the last guy had a deal."

"And what was that, exactly?"

The deal had to do with getting ready to die, which Clarence Buchanan was busy doing when Cody came along. Cody Miller took notice of the desolate surroundings and the golden hook and decided he was fine helping the old man along.

It was Cody who helped Clarence dig the hole, Cody who helped him build the wooden coffin out of slats torn from the hut the old man had lived in most of his life.

"This here gold was my daddy's," Clarence said when the hole was dug and the coffin was built (which amounted to seven Fridays for Cody). He held up the golden hook, the weight of which had trained that left arm into a hammer of incredible strength for fifty years or more. Even at ninety-one, the arm and the hook could rip things apart when the need arose.

"This town ain't never give me or my daddy nothin'. You best bury me with my treasure. Understand?"

Cody Miller nodded, staring into the dark eyes of a withered face. But in the blackest part of his heart lay a hidden secret he had told no one. He had a gold ring on his finger, a treasure of his own that had come into his possession by unsavory means. He turned the ring with the fingers of his other hand and bore down on an evil thought.

No one will know.

On that very day, Clarence Buchanan slumped over in a chair and breathed his last. The gold hook, still attached to Clarence, rested on a decrepit table next to the chair.

Cody rolled the body into the wooden coffin that lay in the hole he'd helped dig. He heard the body of Clarence Buchanan land with the dull thud of death. He took time to lay the body out with care, then he rolled up the sleeve on Clarence Buchanan's left arm. It was an arm no one but Clarence had set eyes on in a very, very long time. The treasure went up the arm farther than Cody could believe—half a foot of gleaming gold—a fortune of serious value. It was held tight to Clarence Buchanan's skin by a wide leather belt, which Cody unstrapped with shaking hands.

The fog had rolled in as night approached, just as it had on the day a hand was crushed so long ago. Cody couldn't be sure if he was shivering from the wet cold or from the fact that he was stealing treasure off a dead man's arm.

As the golden hook came loose and Cody felt the full weight of its value, Clarence Buchanan's last words rang in his ears.

You best bury me with my treasure. Understand?

Cody put the cover on the coffin.

He nailed it shut.

He spent the next hour filling in the dirt.

When he was done, it was night in the woods, and a bitter cold had set in.

He took up his treasure, heavy like a block of iron, and ran.

When he arrived back home, Cody Miller prepared to melt the hook into a block of gold, pack his things, and leave the town of Marshall forever.

We find him now at the makeshift stove, the hook on the floor next to him, the deed about to be done.

WATCH THE
ENDING IF YOU
DARE!

LOG ON NOW TO SEE THE CHILLING CONCLUSION. . . .

315STORIES.COM
PASSWORD: HOOK

ooking for a job was the last thing on Jamie Hanover's mind as she trudged home from school on a chilly, gray afternoon. Jobs in town were scarce, especially for teenagers. Why bother?

It made her first encounter with Miss Pratt all the more surprising.

Miss Pratt was ancient, like a dried flower behind glass, and she was placing a HELP WANTED sign in her window. She looked up, and Jamie saw the clear blue eyes of a much younger woman. When Miss Pratt spoke, Jamie couldn't hear the words from outside, but she could read them on Miss Pratt's thin lips — *Come inside.*

It was easy for Jamie to imagine what she could do with some extra money. She could hang out at the mall with her friends and actually buy something; she could start saving for a car. And so, on that cold November day, Jamie Hanover didn't hesitate. She pushed open the front door, and the twinkling of a bell overhead announced her arrival.

There were floor-to-ceiling shelves everywhere, each one crowded with antiques, battered tools, ancient kitchen appliances, well-loved toys, and old musical instruments. There were piles of books stacked against the shelves, and boxes overflowing with old clothes. Miss Pratt might have been as old as dirt, but she'd used her many years to collect a treasure trove of weird stuff. Jamie had an appreciation for such things, and she was immediately drawn to the idea of working among the countless artifacts fighting for her attention.

"Cold outside?" Miss Pratt asked, shuffling a few steps closer. She set her hand on a stack of comic books and waited for an answer. Her face was a mask of wrinkles and sagging flesh.

"Yes, ma'am," Jamie said loudly. "I saw the sign on the front door, and was wondering about the job. . . ."

"You don't have to yell," Miss Pratt said. "Contrary to popular opinion, I'm not deaf."

Miss Pratt stepped behind the counter and sat carefully on an overstuffed pink chair. There was nowhere for Jamie to sit, so she just stood there, feeling awkward.

"Tell me a little bit about yourself," Miss Pratt said, peering at Jamie through thick-rimmed glasses.

For the next ten minutes, Miss Pratt peppered Jamie with questions. She asked about her grades, her friends, where she went to church, what her parents did, where she lived, the names of her grandparents, and what she liked to do for fun. Finally, the old woman sighed with satisfaction. "Well, Miss Hanover, I think you'll do."

It had all happened so quickly, Jamie didn't quite know what to say. "Uh, thanks, Mrs. . . ."

"You can call me *Miss* Pratt."

"Okay, great. Miss Pratt. When would you like me to start?"

"You already did," Miss Pratt said softly, "but you can go home now. I'll expect you back tomorrow right after school."

Jamie held out her hand, barely able to contain her excitement. "You won't be sorry."

"I hope you're right," Miss Pratt said, leaning forward and clutching Jamie's hand. The bright blue eyes narrowed, and Jamie felt a chill of nervousness. Had she done something wrong? Maybe she hadn't gotten the job after all.

"Promise me you won't take anything without asking."

Jamie jerked her hand away and forced a smile. "I promise," she said.

Whatever second thoughts Jamie might have had were gone by the time she was out the front door. She paused on the sidewalk and smiled. She couldn't believe her good fortune. This job was going to be perfect.

Over the next few weeks, Jamie arrived promptly at the Once Upon a Time Antique Store. She learned early on that Miss Pratt wasn't a typical boss. She often barely talked to Jamie, giving her a few simple instructions and then letting her work on her own while she napped. When there were no customers — which was most of the time — Jamie kept busy cleaning, dusting, sorting, and organizing. Jamie soon decided that "antique" was just a fancy name for overpriced junk.

With one exception: the jewelry display cases, which were overflowing with rings, necklaces, earrings, and fancy hat pins. *Wow* was all Jamie could say when she first saw these treasures.

Jamie couldn't seem to spend enough time in that part of the store. There was always another ring to polish, or another bracelet to scrub, or another egg-size diamond, ruby, or emerald to admire. Of course, it was all cheap costume jewelry. But Jamie thought these items were fantastic just the same.

And then it happened.

One afternoon, Jamie stumbled across the most beautiful ring she'd ever seen. It was lying in the bottom of a box that had been stuck beneath one of the display cases. She held the ring up to the light and marveled at the way it shimmered. She polished it until it sparkled like new, then reluctantly placed it inside the display case where she could keep an eye on it.

From that moment on, Jamie couldn't get the ring out of her head.

A week or so after finding it, Jamie happened to be dusting the jewelry display case. She lingered when she came close to the ring, glancing up to make sure the old woman was asleep in her chair. Then she slipped the ring on her finger, surprised by how perfectly it fit.

Miss Pratt's warning rang in her ears: *Promise me you won't take anything without asking.*

It isn't stealing, Jamie decided, her hands trembling with excitement. *I'll just be borrowing it for a little while. Miss Pratt won't even notice.*

Jamie slipped the ring off and put it in her pocket, then scurried off to sort through a box of old toys on the other side of the store. She didn't notice the faint movement of the old woman's head, or the hint of a smile that touched her lips.

Two days later, Jamie took another ring. It was almost as beautiful as the first one. And that night, just before turning out the light and crawling into bed, she stared at the two rings sitting side by side on top of her dresser. *I'm just* borrowing *the rings,* she reminded herself.

A week later, the two rings had been joined on Jamie's dresser by a gold bracelet, an antique watch, and a jewel-encrusted hairpin. By now, Jamie had completely forgotten about Miss Pratt's warning, and as she worked that afternoon, she was trying to decide whether to add to her jewelry collection by "borrowing" a gold necklace with a ruby pendant. Maybe she'd just take it home, try it on, and decide. . . .

"Jamie, would you come here, please?" Miss Pratt called out.

Uh-oh.

Startled, Jamie dropped the necklace. For a heartbeat, she thought about running for the door. But then the impulse passed.

"Yes, ma'am?" Jamie answered, pasting a cheery smile on her face.

As usual, Miss Pratt was sitting in the over-stuffed chair. She waited for Jamie to come close and then pointed to an old-fashioned mirror leaning up against the wall. It was oval and large, about three feet tall.

"I think you deserve a reward for all your hard work," she said, her blue eyes glittering behind her glasses. "A beautiful girl needs a beautiful mirror."

"Oh, you shouldn't have," Jamie said with relief.

Miss Pratt didn't seem to be listening as she went on about the gift. "I call this mirror the reflecting pool. I suspect it may have had other names, but I was never able to discover them."

"Thanks, Miss Pratt," Jamie said, eyeing the mirror. It looked heavy. "What did you call it again?"

"The reflecting pool . . ."

Weird, Jamie thought.

When Jamie got home, she set the mirror on her dresser. She had to admit it was kind of cool to look at, almost mesmerizing. It seemed to reflect things perfectly one moment, and then the next, the reflection would change and shift as if the mirror were made of water. Jamie hopped off her bed and brushed her fingers lightly across the mirror's surface, holding her breath as she did it. She half expected them to come back dripping wet. But it was only a mirror, after all.

Just before she turned off her light, she gazed fondly at the jewelry lined up in front of the mirror. "Lucky me," she said softly.

The next morning, Jamie rolled out of bed, yawned loudly, and absentmindedly walked to the dresser. She reached out, searching for the things she'd taken.

"What the—?" she whispered.

The rings were gone.

Jamie searched behind the mirror, and then dropped to her hands and knees and felt under the dresser.

Nothing.

Where could they be? She had no idea. Her room was on the second floor, the window painted shut long ago. She felt a flutter of panic as she remembered the old woman's warning once more: *Promise me you won't take anything without asking.*

"This is bad," she said.

Her mom's voice drifted upstairs. "You'd better hurry or you'll be late."

"Be right there," Jamie answered. She spent a few more minutes looking and then quickly finished getting ready for school.

Jamie's day dragged on as if it would never end. She struggled to stay focused as science, then math, then English passed in a haze. All she could think about was Miss Pratt's wrinkled face as she repeated those awful words over and over.

Don't take anything without asking. Don't! Don't! Don't!

When the bell finally rang, she was too afraid to go to work. She ran straight home, dropped her backpack on the floor, and flew up the stairs to her room. What she found made her feel faint. Not only were the rings still missing, now the bracelet was gone, too.

"What am I going to do?" she whispered out loud. She gathered up the watch and the hairpin, placed them in a sock, and then lifted up a heating vent on the floor and stuffed the sock as far back into the duct as she could reach. They'd be safe there.

After dinner, Jamie's parents went out for a movie. By the time Jamie returned to her room, she was alone in a dark house on a dark night. She entered her room as if it were no longer her own. It didn't feel safe anymore. It felt like something was in there, waiting for her, watching her. She opened the vent on the floor and pulled out the sock. It was empty.

First the rings, then the bracelet, and now the watch. All gone!

The only item that remained was the fancy hairpin, which had somehow found its way to the dresser, where it sat next to a random collection of objects beneath the mirror.

"How did you get all the way over there?" Jamie said, walking quietly across the room.

When she arrived at the dresser, she stared at the hairpin.

Then she felt a strange wind begin to blow in the room. Where was it coming from?

LOG ON NOW TO SEE THE CHILLING CONCLUSION. . . .

315STORIES.COM
PASSWORD: MIRROR

A **3:15** Original Story

Episode 03

MR. MASON'S JARS

FOR AN AUDIO INTRODUCTION TO THIS
STORY, VISIT WWW.315STORIES.COM

PASSWORD: WESTMONT

ost middle schools have at least one teacher who students avoid at all costs. The reason for the avoidance is usually one of three things:

The teacher is horribly mean and grouchy.

The teacher is so boring and monotonous that a forty-five minute class feels like forty-five days of mental torture.

The teacher is a very close talker with monstrously bad breath.

At Westmont Middle School, Mr. Mason is that teacher. And what's worse, he is all three of these terrible things wrapped up in one extraordinarily awful person. Students scatter when they see him coming down the hall in his musty wool sweaters, hoping not to be breathed on.

"Is that him?"

Molly didn't answer the new kid. It was bad enough she had Mr. Mason's eighth-grade science class, and she sure didn't want to draw any attention to herself as he walked by. Unfortunately, it was too late.

"Is that who?" Mr. Mason said, stopping behind Molly and the new kid, leaning down in their direction. Mr.

Mason was also tall, with a woolly-looking gray beard and sharp eyes. He gazed down at Molly as his breath nearly melted her face off.

"Hi, Mr. Mason," said Molly. "This is Troy. He's new."

Troy was a rambling talker and had the misfortune of not realizing Mr. Mason hated talkative kids.

"Whoa, cool beard, Mr. Mason! I wish I could grow one of those. Maybe someday."

"You're annoying. And loud. Please say you don't have third-period science."

"Oh, I have it all right!" said Troy, holding out a package of Life Savers. "Mint?"

Mr. Mason snatched the roll of mints from Troy in one quick motion and scowled down at the boy. "These are not allowed in my class. No candy, gum, or *talking*."

Molly started to drift away as slowly and carefully as she could, but Mr. Mason's gaze landed on her and she froze in place.

"I've got my eye on both of you. I smell trouble."

"I think that might be your breath, Mr. Mason. It's really the only smellable thing in this general space."

Mr. Mason's face went white. His teeth moved inside his head as he ground them back and forth, and his eyes began to bulge. Just as it looked like he was going to blow his top, he turned violently and walked away.

"What did you have to go and do that for?" said Molly, punching the new kid on the shoulder.

"You punch like a girl," said Troy.

"I *am* a girl, you moron! And do yourself a favor: Don't get on Mr. Mason's radar. He's creepy. And he hates kids like you."

"Mr. Mason hates cool kids?"

"Ha. Ha," Molly said, backing toward her next class as the bell rang. "Don't say I didn't warn you. Guys like you take his class and they're never the same after."

"What does that even mean? And more importantly, would you be my girlfriend?"

Molly rolled her eyes, but she also couldn't help smiling a little. Troy was cute and she'd met him first, before any of the other girls could claim his attention. Her smile fell away as she thought about Troy provoking Mr. Mason with his goofy sense of humor.

"Just be quiet in Mr. Mason's class, okay? I mean it."

But Troy was already heading in the other direction, waving at her and saying, "Relax, girlfriend. I'll buy you a soft pretzel at lunch. Meet me?"

The question hung in the air, then Molly nodded and smiled back, a bigger smile this time, and she turned into a sea of kids racing between first and second period.

When Molly arrived in Mr. Mason's class an hour later, she tried to sit next to Troy in the back row.

"You," Mr. Mason said from the front of the room, pointing a long finger at her. "Up here, in front."

The front row of Mr. Mason's class was the worst location in the entire school. Stale coffee breath hung on every word Mr. Mason said, and every one of those words was world-class BORING.

"Yo, Mr. Mason," Troy said from the back of the class, raising his hand but not waiting to be called on.

Oh no, thought Molly.

"What kind of cool stuff do you keep in those jars?" Troy asked.

Everyone in the class sat quiet and still. No one made a sound as Troy pointed to a row of glass jars sitting on a table behind Mr. Mason. They were the old kind, mason jars, with gold tin lids. Each jar appeared to be filled with goopy liquid of one color or another.

A strange and unpleasant smile crept onto Mr. Mason's face.

"If I don't call on you, you don't speak," he said, walking between the desks until he stood in front of Troy. He leaned down close and breathed into the boy's face. "Understood?"

"You should really try those mints you took from me, Mr. Mason. They taste pretty good."

A few of the boys chuckled softly, but Mr. Mason stood bolt upright and glared in every direction. Silence enveloped the room.

"I demand order in this classroom," he bellowed, then stared down at Troy.

"I gotcha," said Troy. "Order it is! No more disorder from this guy. I'm *Mr.* Order. You can count on m—"

"Not another word!" said Mr. Mason. He rubbed his

temple, feeling a migraine coming on, and in the quiet of his black heart, he planned to deal with *Troy* in the usual way he treated this particular kind of student.

Mr. Mason walked back to the front of the room, all the while looking at his glass jars.

When class was over, Molly waited for Troy in the hallway, then they walked to the lunchroom together.

"You are one dumb kid," she said, shaking her head. "I told you not to do that! Why couldn't you just play it cool?"

"Awww, you worry too much. But you're darn cute, so I'll let it slide."

Molly blushed. *Darn cute?* She liked the sound of that. Molly pulled Troy down onto the floor in the corner of the cafeteria where they could talk privately before anyone else joined them.

"Troy, listen to me," she said softly. "You have to cool it in that class. I mean it."

"Why would I want to do that?" asked Troy. "I'm like his favorite student already. He digs me."

"Why would you say that?"

"Because," said Troy, standing so he could go get two

soft pretzels. "He said so. He even invited me to stop in and check out his secret jars after school."

Molly pulled Troy down hard—in fact, she was a little concerned when she heard his shirt rip a tiny bit.

"Sorry, that's—my bad," she said, but Troy just smiled as she pointed to a guy walking across the cafeteria. "You see him? That's Dale. He used to be a lot like you. Then he stopped by Mr. Mason's class after school."

Troy looked up and saw an eighth grader moving slowly toward the bathroom. He looked a little like a zombie—or, possibly, someone who was half asleep.

"He looks tired," said Troy.

"He's not *tired*. He's just—*different*. He's super-quiet all the time. But he never used to be like that. He was a loudmouth in Mr. Mason's class. Like you."

"You're saying I'm a loudmouth?"

"Well, yeah, kind of."

"How cute. Our first fight. Let's celebrate with some soft pretzels!"

Before Molly could stop him, Troy was up and away, bounding across the cafeteria until he met up with really-tired-zombie-looking Dale. Molly watched as Troy stuck out his finger and poked Dale gently on the shoulder. Dale mumbled hello and kept walking as Troy looked back at Molly and mouthed the word *weird!*

Molly spent the rest of lunch trying to convince Troy not to visit Mr. Mason's class after school.

But it didn't matter.

Troy was Troy, which was to say, he wasn't going to miss a chance to check out those jars.

"Whoa. That is one stinky jar of *something*. Puts your breath to shame."

Mr. Mason twitched at the insult.

"Doesn't it, though?" Mr. Mason agreed. It was killing him to be nice to Troy.

The two had been opening some of the jars together for a few minutes.

"What's in there? No, wait, don't tell me — it's a human finger floating in a pool of fish guts!"

"You're a very imaginative young man, Troy. Has anyone ever told you that?"

"All the time. But seriously, what's in there?"

Mr. Mason put the jar back where he'd gotten it.

"Let's just say what's in that jar will melt the gum off the bottom of a chair in a matter of seconds."

"Cool."

"But not as cool as what's in *this* jar," said Mr. Mason, reaching back and picking up a glass jar filled with something sloshy and purple. "This is the *real* stuff. My own scientific blend of . . ."

Mr. Mason deliberately let his words trail off. He liked to let his unruly students guess at the contents.

"Your own blend of *awesome*, right?"

A typical answer, full of annoying vigor and void of any intellect. Mr. Mason touched his temple, a very bad headache having moved behind his eyeballs.

Not to worry, he thought. *This, too, shall pass.*

"The thing about this one . . . ," said Mr. Mason, sliding the jar in front of Troy, who was eager to get his hands on it. "Well, the thing is, what's inside will escape if you leave it open too long. You have to be careful about opening it."

"You have a live little dude in there?" asked Troy.

Mr. Mason nodded conspiratorially.

"Yes, a live little dude."

"Like a frog or a giant swimming bug?"

"Something like that," said Mr. Mason, using his friendliest voice even as Troy was annoying him half to death. "You'll need to get close, open the jar just a little, and peek inside. Carefully. Do you think you could do that?"

Troy grabbed the jar and slid it close to his face.

"This close enough?" he asked, so excited he could barely stand the wait.

"Maybe . . . a *little* closer."

Troy moved his face a little closer.

"Has anyone else ever seen what's inside this jar?" asked Troy.

"Absolutely not," said Mr. Mason. "You'll be the first."

"Wow. That's like the coolest thing ever. You're already my favorite teacher, Mr. Mason."

For the blink of an eye, Mr. Mason thought better of his plan. Troy had seemed so annoying, so loud and obnoxious. But now, at the moment of his undoing, Troy had said something rare to Mr. Mason.

You're my favorite teacher.

Mr. Mason hadn't heard those words in . . . well, he'd *never* heard those words.

But it was too late.

Troy had opened the jar and peeked inside.

The deed was done and it could never be taken back.

Molly, who had come to wait by the door in the hallway outside, heard a loud and frightening sound.

She'd heard it before.

They all had.

And somehow she just knew.

When she saw Troy again, he wouldn't be the same person.

WATCH THE ENDING IF YOU DARE!

LOG ON NOW TO SEE THE CHILLING CONCLUSION. . . .

315STORIES.COM
PASSWORD: ALCHEMY

Episode 04

A **3:15** Original Story

THE LIFT

A late-season storm bringing a foot of fresh powder to the mountains was a rarity. When it happened during the middle of the week and forced the schools in the small town of Buckley to close, it was a gift from the snowboard gods.

At least that's how Adam Thomas and Dylan Smith looked at it.

They were obsessed with snowboarding. When they weren't snowboarding, they were dreaming about snowboarding. And when it was summer, they read boarding magazines and watched boarding videos. They even went so far as to build a ramp in Adam's backyard that ended in a pile of wood chips. It was a rough landing, but it helped pass the time until the snow fell again.

Still, nothing compared to the real deal. Adam and Dylan weren't about to miss the opportunity for a day on the mountain.

Unless, of course, Adam got them killed first.

"Dude, slow down!" Dylan yelled above the music blasting out of the car's half-blown-out speakers. "The snow's not going anywhere."

The car was old but it went plenty fast, and as usual, Adam was taking the slick corners quicker than Dylan was comfortable with. He held on to the door handle as Adam threw the Honda into another slide around a blind corner on the narrow, snow-covered road.

"No worries, bro!" shouted Adam. "I got this!"

As the car drifted into the other lane, Adam screamed with joy and honked the horn. He punched the accelerator, and the tired engine roared in protest. The studded snow tires bit into the softer snow; the car clawed back into its lane.

A moment later, a delivery truck blew by in a hurricane of snow and debris.

"Five seconds!" Dylan yelled. "Just five little seconds and we'd have been face-to-face with that thing."

Adam didn't seem to even hear Dylan.

"Don't you feel it, bro? The mountain is calling us. And today, I promise you, I'm gonna land that 360."

Dylan didn't contradict him. He wasn't stupid. Adam could brag all he wanted, and Dylan would let it slide because of one all-important fact: Adam had the wheels. Without Adam, Dylan was stuck—no wheels, no snowboarding. And Dylan had some serious tricks of his own he wanted to bring out of the backyard and up to the mountain. He reached forward and turned down the volume on the stereo.

"Just take it easy," he said. "The snow's still gonna be there whether we arrive in ten minutes or twenty. And either way, you know I'm gonna rule the mountain."

Because here was the thing: Adam might have had the wheels, but Dylan had the mad skills. He'd landed his first 360 two seasons earlier, and Adam had been eating powder ever since. Being younger by a year only made it sweeter.

"Remember what happened to Bobby Miller?" Adam asked, punching in the clutch and quickly downshifting as they came to a hairpin turn. He wasn't really asking, Dylan knew. This came up all the time with Adam, and Dylan had learned to roll with it.

"Yeah, yeah. Whatever."

"I'm serious," Adam said with a raised eyebrow. "He was the hot-shot boarder. I mean, he could do stuff that you could only dream about doing."

"Is that right?" Dylan said, not sure if he'd been insulted or if it was just Adam blowing more hot air his way.

"He was awesome. You know he was. Until he ran into something he couldn't beat."

"A tree," said Dylan, as if he'd heard it all before (which he had—many times). "I know the story, Adam. It's not like it's new or anything."

Adam took his eyes off the road and stared at Dylan.

"Dead. Yep. According to the stories, he was dead before he hit the ground—I mean, the snow. Broken neck."

Dylan felt a chill flutter down his back. That part of the story always bugged him, even if he *had* heard it a bunch of times. He turned up the heat in the car and gazed out the window.

As Adam slid the car around another curve, Dylan caught a glimpse of a person walking way off in the woods. He was holding his snowboard in one hand, dragging it on the ground. Whoever it was glanced over his shoulder as the car passed.

"Hey, did you see that guy?"

"You saw a person?" Adam said sarcastically. "Out there?"

"I'm telling you, there was someone standing out there. We should go back."

"It was a tree," Adam said. "Or Bigfoot. Just chill."

"What if he needed our help?"

"Then he woulda been standing on the edge of the road! You're seeing things." He gave Dylan a wolfish grin. "Or maybe you just saw *Bobby Miller*?" He began to hum the theme song from that old shark movie *Jaws*.

Dylan felt that chill again. "Very funny. Just drive."

"I know these two guys at school," said Adam, anticipation rising in his voice. "On their final run down the hill last year, just as it was starting to get dark, they were chased. *Chased*, dude! By something . . . not quite human . . ."

"You're starting to freak me out," Dylan said.

Adam shrugged. "They said it was like a black shadow on a board, riding right through the trees, doing all sorts of bizarre tricks. You've gotta wonder. . . . Bobby Miller always acted like he owned the place. And from what I heard, he didn't like anyone showing him up."

Dylan shook his head. "I don't believe in that kinda stuff."

"Yeah?" said Adam. "Well, maybe you should. My advice? If you're gonna tear it up, I'd get off the slopes before the sun starts to set. Just to be safe."

It was nearly noon before Adam's Honda slid into the parking lot at Bluewood Ski Resort. They grabbed their gear and snowboards, trudged up to the lodge, and got their day passes. Ten minutes later, they were standing in some of the best powder they'd ever seen. It was amazing snow—perfect for testing out new tricks. It'd be like landing in six feet of cotton candy.

"Welcome to Bluewood, boys," the lift attendant said as they waited in the line.

They knew this guy by sight. He was one of the regular workers who crawled out of some cave or bar or mountain cabin every fall, worked through the winter, and then disappeared again. He was dressed in oil-stained snowmobile coveralls and he had a ratty beard that looked like dirty dishwater. *Clifton* was stitched across the front of the overalls. Dylan had never been sure if it was his first name or last.

"Incredible snow, Clifton!" Adam yelled.

"Powder as far as the eye can see," Clifton agreed. "Enjoy it while it lasts. S'pose to warm up tomorrow, then it'll turn to mush."

One day of powder, that was it. Dylan and Adam looked at each other and knew they had to make the most of it.

Clifton smiled, leaned in close to the boys, and said, "A smart man might make sure he's off the mountain before ol' Bobby decides to take a few runs." Clifton's cackle followed Adam and Dylan as their chair started up the hill.

"What a freak," Dylan muttered under his breath.

"He's harmless," Adam said. "And funny. So, the usual plan?"

"Sounds good to me," Dylan said with a shrug.

"The usual plan" meant that if they happened to get separated, they'd make sure to keep in touch using the walkie-talkies they both carried.

In fact, Dylan usually went out of his way to ditch Adam. He actually preferred snowboarding alone. There was nothing quite like coming across a slope covered with fresh powder and knowing that he didn't have to share it with anyone.

Adam managed to keep up for the first two runs, but on the third, Dylan saw Adam flip over his nose and disappear into a cloud of snow near the edge of the trees. Instead of stopping, Dylan pointed his board straight downhill and took off.

Hours passed and the boys saw each other here and there, but Dylan was so on and the powder was so great, he just had to take the toughest routes and get as much big air as possible. Somewhere around five P.M., with only enough remaining light for a run or two, Dylan's walkie-talkie sounded off.

"Where are ya, dude?"

"Almost at the top," Dylan answered. "You okay?"

"I had an awesome wipeout. You shoulda seen it!"

"Yeah, sorry I missed it," Dylan half lied. "If we don't

meet up, I'll catch you at the lodge after the last run. I'm gonna try and get in a couple more."

"Let's run it together. I'll meet you at the bottom."

Dylan wasn't so sure. The good snow would be gone by the next day, and anyway, they weren't coming back up until who-knew-when. He needed to make the most of what little time he had left.

"Let's just meet at the lodge, if that's cool," said Dylan.

A long pause on the walkie-talkie followed, and then Adam's voice returned.

"Okay . . . yeah, sure. I might wait for you at the lift, anyway."

He sounded disappointed.

Dylan felt a little bad for ditching, but the feeling quickly passed as he raced down the mountain.

The next two runs seemed almost like a dream. Dylan was having the best afternoon of his life. He was snowboarding like those guys you see in Warren Miller movies. He kept finding open glens with fresh snow, and jumps, drops, and ledges that let him try out all of his tricks.

In fact, Dylan almost wished Adam — or someone — had been around so they could see how awesome he was doing. But the mountain was starting to empty of people as it got colder and closer to dark.

When Dylan stopped to catch his breath after a particularly great landing, he suddenly had a strange feeling — like he was being watched. He scanned the trees and the slopes behind him, and felt that familiar chill in his bones.

But he was completely alone.

After a long minute of absolute stillness, Dylan spied someone weaving fearlessly through a tight stand of trees and, feeling sort of spooked, took off after him. But when he lost sight of the guy and tried to follow his path through the trees, he couldn't find any tracks in the snow.

Weird.

It was closing in on darkness when Dylan coasted to the lift. There was no line, only Clifton stomping his boots to keep warm.

"Technically, the lift is closed," said Clifton. He looked

every which way, as if the cops might show up and haul him away for letting a kid ride up one last time. "You wanna go once more, I'll look the other way."

As Dylan started to dig out his walkie-talkie, Adam came barreling past and pulled to a stop right where he'd be able to hop onto the next chair.

"Hey, man! Haven't seen you in a while." Dylan was actually relieved to see his friend. He'd been on his own long enough; it would be good to travel to the top one more time with his buddy. Dylan lined up next to Adam and waited for the two-person chair to swing around and pick them up.

"Last run!" said Clifton, waving them onto the lift. "See you at the lodge."

Adam kept his helmet and goggles on as Dylan sat down beside him. He seemed upset.

"Some good runs today?" asked Dylan, but Adam just stared off into the trees without answering. It was darker and colder on the lift as it snaked through the tall trees. Dylan looked up the long line of empty chairs in front of him and shivered as he was buffeted by a gust of wind.

He was starting to think this might not have been the best idea.

"Let's stick together on this one, okay?" Dylan asked his friend. Adam stayed silent, unmoving, and Dylan started to think maybe he'd taken one too many runs on his own. Maybe he'd been a little too brash about his skills.

"Sorry I ditched you today," Dylan said, his teeth chattering.

And then a strange thing happened.

Dylan's walkie-talkie started blaring in his pocket. He fumbled into his jacket and pressed the button on the side.

"Adam?" he said, looking at the figure slumped in the chair next to him.

There was a long, static-filled pause.

And then Adam's voice, coming through the walkie-talkie.

"Hey, if you can hear me, I'm waiting for you at the lodge. You there? Hello?"

"Yeah," Dylan said very quietly, a tremble in his voice as the cold started to clamp around his limbs. "I'm heading up for one more run."

Another long pause, then finally Adam was back, quieter this time.

"Just get off the mountain, okay? It's getting dark."

Dylan twisted around in his seat and looked at the line of empty chairs going all the way to the bottom. Clifton was gone.

Everyone was gone.

It was like Dylan was the only living thing on the mountain.

Him and whoever—or *whatever*—was sitting next to him.

A 3:15 Original Story

Episode 05

NIGHT RIDER

FOR AN AUDIO INTRODUCTION TO THIS STORY, VISIT WWW.315STORIES.COM

PASSWORD: JUNEBUG

homas wasn't interested in having a girlfriend. Between school, his job at the skateboard shop, and longboard racing, he couldn't be bothered. At least, that's what he told himself.

But that all changed one gray, blustery Sunday afternoon in late October.

As Thomas and his buddy, Anthony, were slaloming down the hill on Oak Street on their longboards, they were suddenly passed as if they were standing still.

"What the—?" Thomas managed. Someone had just rolled by them—someone on a longboard, going insanely fast. That alone was enough to get Thomas's attention. But there was something more.

It wasn't a dude on the longboard. It was a girl.

She looked over her shoulder at Thomas and smiled, and he felt something like an electric jolt—then almost tumbled off his board.

"Who the heck was *that*?" he yelled, sliding to a stop and watching the girl rocket down the hill.

"New girl at school," Anthony said, pulling up next to Thomas. "A real thrill seeker, if the rumors are true. My sister said her name is Amy . . . but forget about it. She's way out of your league, bro."

"Might not matter," Thomas said, starting down the hill again. "She's in trouble."

Amy was about to cross four lanes of traffic.

"Dude, this is gonna be bad," Anthony said.

As Amy approached the intersection, she crouched down to gain more speed. Thomas closed his eyes. He couldn't watch. There was a scream of brakes and wailing car horns. Thomas automatically reached for the cell phone in his pocket, ready to punch in 911.

"Awesome," Anthony said, laughing and slapping Thomas on the back.

Thomas still couldn't look. "She's dead, right?"

"Check it out," Anthony said.

Thomas opened his eyes and saw Amy on the other side of traffic, arms raised over her head, riding her longboard down the center of the street like she owned it. When she looked back up the hill and waved, there was no doubt about it. Thomas just knew. She was waving at *him*.

"I've gotta meet her," Thomas murmured as he watched Amy disappear around a corner. "Can your sister get me her number?"

Anthony raced ahead and called back, "She's bad news. You sure you want to deal with that?"

Thomas kicked his board down the hill and caught up with Anthony as they turned a sharp corner, avoiding the peril Amy had just navigated.

"I'm sure. Just ask her, okay?"

"It's your funeral, man," Anthony said with a shake of his head. "I'll see what I can do."

Thomas couldn't restrain himself. "Yes!" he shouted with a fist pump. He pointed his deck downhill and followed after Anthony.

The next morning, even before Thomas was out of bed, he sent Anthony a text: HEY BRO GOT HER #?

He sent another text five minutes later: U THERE?

And then another five minutes after that: WHASUP?

A dozen texts later, he finally got a reply from Anthony: PATIENCE IS A VIRTUE.

Being patient was the last thing on Thomas's mind. He couldn't help it. There was something about Amy that he just couldn't shake. He *had* to meet her.

Thomas forced himself to take a deep breath. Anthony was his friend. He wouldn't let him down.

The long-awaited text from Anthony came during the middle of second period. It included Amy's number and a message: U OWE ME BRO. BE CAREFUL.

WHATEVER U NEED! Thomas texted back immediately, barely able to contain his excitement. But then he realized he had a new problem. And this one was way serious.

What was he going to text her that didn't come across as lame or stupid?

He tried out and then rejected dozens of texts between classes. When he noticed he was starting to repeat himself, he decided it was time to just go for it.

He typed in the message: HEY AMY. GOT UR # FROM A FRIEND. SAW U ON OAK ST HILL ON SUN. He held his breath, and then tapped the send button.

A few minutes later, he felt his phone vibrate. It was her. And instead of telling him to drop dead, she asked: WHAT DID U THINK?

"How cool is that!" Thomas said to himself. He quickly replied: WOW. JUST W.O.W.

There was a flurry of text messages after that:

WHAT'S UR NAME?

THOMAS

U THE CHICKEN I SAW YESTERDAY?

YEP

THOUGHT U AND FRIEND WOULD FOLLOW??? LOL

WE AREN'T NUTS

WIMPS?

YEAH. LOL. WANNA MEET AND TALK RACING BOARDS AND STUFF?

WHEN?

TONIGHT. 6?

WHERE?

JUNE BUG.

IS THIS A DATE?

June Bug was a café downtown with overpriced coffee,

a good place to chill and get to know each other. Thomas arrived at Mrs. Sykes's science class and slumped into his seat without answering. IS THIS A DATE? He stared at the words, not sure how to answer, then put his phone away as Mrs. Sykes introduced a video they were going to watch about DNA and the human genome project. When the class finally let out, he had decided on his answer.

HOW ABOUT WE CALL IT A START? He sent the text and crossed his fingers.

And then he waited.

By lunchtime, Amy still hadn't replied. Thomas was so nervous he couldn't eat. He spent the entire time wandering around the cafeteria, hoping to catch a glimpse of her. He wasn't sure they even shared the same lunch break, but it couldn't hurt to look.

When he walked past Anthony, his friend took one glance at him and just rolled his eyes. "You're on another planet, man," he said.

Toward the end of sixth period, Thomas still hadn't received a reply from Amy. *Guess that tells me what she thought of my answer,* he thought morosely. *Stupid.*

That's when his cell phone buzzed. He was afraid to look at it, but he took a deep breath and held the screen where he could see it, just out of the teacher's sight.

SEE U THERE!

"That's what I'm talking about!" he yelled. And then he realized that everyone in class was staring at him.

"Is there a problem, Thomas?" his teacher, Mr. Gordon, barked.

He was saved by the bell . . . literally. As the kids in the classroom scrambled to their feet, Mr. Gordon just waved dismissively at Thomas.

Whew.

Normally, Thomas didn't think much about what he was wearing. But that night was special, so he decided to head home before the date and raid the laundry room for clean clothes. He put on his lucky jeans, a clean unwrinkled T-shirt, and the new Silverfish hoodie he'd received as a birthday present from his parents. He checked his face, ran a hand through his hair, grabbed his board, and was on his way to June Bug by five thirty.

What was typically a fifteen-minute ride on his longboard took just seven.

Thomas grabbed an empty table by the front window and immediately noticed a server giving him the hairy eyeball.

"I'm waiting for my date," he explained.

"Goody for you," she said sarcastically. "What can I get you *while* you wait?"

Thomas was in such a great mood, her sarcasm didn't even bother him. "How about a mocha latte for starters . . . with lots of whipped cream."

Halfway through his mocha, Thomas glanced nervously at the clock on the wall. 5:50. Still plenty of time. He double-checked to make sure his phone was on, and then filled the time by going over some questions he wanted to ask her. Where are you from? When did you start longboard racing? Got a favorite brand of wheel? How did you manage to cross that intersection without having a car drive over you?

The next time Thomas looked at the clock, it was six. The café was getting crowded. He tugged at the strings on his hoodie and stared out the window. Sirens howled faintly in the distance. The streetlights outside looked like balls of glowing cotton candy against a mist that covered everything with a gray smear.

He saw someone move in the mist, and his heart began beating faster with anticipation—but then an old guy with a walker stepped out of the dark and into the pale pool of light beyond the window.

"Anything else?" The server stood next to the table, glaring at him. He could tell what she was thinking: *Order something else or get outta here.*

"Uh, yeah, how about another mocha?"

The server rolled her eyes and turned on her heels.

By 6:10, Thomas was starting to get worried. He pulled out his phone and sent Amy a text: WHERE R U?

And then he waited.

While his heart sank slowly toward his toes, he didn't look at the clock; he didn't even touch his mocha. The minutes slipped by, and he wondered how he was going to explain this to Anthony: *I'm a stupid idiot and you were right. She is out of my league. . . .*

When Thomas's phone buzzed, he was so startled he nearly knocked over his drink. He checked the number. It was Amy. And then he noticed the message. It made absolutely no sense: COLD SO FALLS THE VACANT NIGHT49.

Thomas's hands were trembling as he replied: ?????????

Ten minutes later, there was still no reply from Amy.

If Thomas had chosen to throw in the towel and go home, it might have ended right there. Hurt feelings, but that's all. But he continued to wait for Amy. He ordered dessert, barely touched it, checked his phone ten more times. Finally, after what felt like hours, he glanced out the front window — and there was Amy racing by on her longboard. When their eyes met, her face stretched into a grin, but she didn't stop. . . .

Thomas hesitated — something about that smile made him shiver — but then his unease faded. He dug out a twenty-dollar bill, tossed it on the table, grabbed his longboard, and dashed for the door. Once outside, he dropped his board onto the sidewalk, and in one quick motion, he was in hot pursuit.

He couldn't let her go. He just couldn't.

"Amy!" he yelled. "Amy! Wait up. It's me . . . !"

WATCH THE ENDING IF YOU DARE!

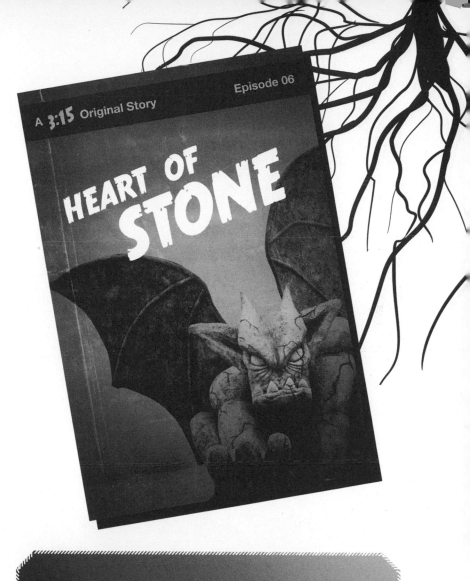

FOR AN AUDIO INTRODUCTION TO THIS
STORY, VISIT WWW.315STORIES.COM

PASSWORD: GARGOYLE

Emma Franklin is eleven, but several of her besties are twelve, and one of them, Sarah, is actually thirteen. Emma suspects that some of her own pretty remarkable maturity comes from being city-born and city-bred, right from Day One. Unlike Sarah, for instance, who used to live in the suburbs.

There's only one way in which Emma feels — privately — just a little bit less sophisticated than some of the kids her age: She's very afraid of a certain something.

It has to do with the fact that her family's apartment is in an older building. The style of architecture, at least according to Hugh, the doorman, is Beaux Arts (he pronounces it "Bozart"), which means absolutely nothing to her. When she was younger, she was convinced it had something to do with clowns or at least the name Bozo. Or maybe Mozart, the famous (dead) composer. Anyway, Bozart doesn't have anything to do with those things. The reason the style of building is important is because sometimes, on Beaux Arts buildings, you get statues up on the ledges — creepy, crouching creatures known as gargoyles.

As it turns out, there's one just about fifteen feet to the side of Emma's window. It's made of stone and it's very old. Some of its face has been worn away by the weather. Imagine a wolf crossed with a toad sitting on its hind legs, all lumpy and gross, and then give it the claws of a sloth and the snout of a weasel. Then make it work out at the gym until it's all muscle-y, and you have a good idea of what this gargoyle looks like: scary.

Really. Really. Scary.

Emma's sister, Janie, has a window, but hers looks out to the side, at the building across the street. Even though Emma's view is the entire reason she begged her parents to give her this room, she asked Janie if she wanted to trade a year ago.

"You'd have the most amazing view in the whole city," Emma promised.

Janie wasn't buying it. "You're trying to trick me," she accused, with those annoying little eyes. "You don't want to have the monster outside your window anymore."

Very helpful, Emma thought, then tried again.

"Sometimes being generous is its own reward. This

would be my gift to you, as my perfect younger sister: a magnificent view."

"No, thank you."

So Emma was stuck with the gargoyle.

There's an identical one on the opposite corner of the building, but you can't see it from Emma's window. You can't even see the one on Emma's side if you're just hanging out in her room or sitting on the bed. But if you walk right up to the window and look to the right, there it is.

Here's what happens at bedtime: Emma checks her homework folder to make sure there's no surprise drudgery from any evil teachers, then she locks Janie out of the bathroom until she can tell Janie's about to pee her pants and go tell their parents, and then she puts on her pajamas and combs her hair. The weirdest part is what she does next, and has done ever since they moved into this apartment: She looks out the window to make sure the gargoyle is still there.

It's not like she's four and still believes in Santa Claus and unicorns. She just likes knowing that it's still perched there, not moving, not turning around, not going anywhere. Just staring out over the city like a watchdog. Which is what she read somewhere they're supposed to do.

If she's being totally honest, Emma would have to admit there have been quite a few times when she's had to get up in the middle of the night and check to make sure the gargoyle was still there. But this is definitely the kind of secret you have to keep to yourself; there's no one she could tell this to who wouldn't be tempted, at *some* point, to blab it to everyone for a laugh at her expense.

Tonight is like every other night. Janie is already in bed, not being allowed to stay up late the way Emma is. The house is quiet, with her mom and dad already snoring in front of some reality show.

There's no homework tonight. All Emma's friends have hypervigilant parents who restrict their phones in the evening, so even though Emma's parents don't do that, there's no one to talk to or text with.

Nothing to do but go to sleep.

And check the gargoyle.

She sits for a moment on the edge of the bed. The thing is, it really is a nice view. There are several blocks of buildings that are shorter than their apartment building, so she can see a good distance. Her favorite things to look at are the water towers. It seems so old-fashioned, so weird, that buildings would keep water up on the roof. It seems to Emma that water should come out of the ground, out of a pipe that's hooked up somewhere, or out of a river. She'll have to Google that someday. Figure out what that's about.

This is what it's like for Emma before it's time to go to sleep. She tries to fill her mind with mundane, useless things like rivers and Ping-Pong—whatever she can come up with to keep her mind off the you-know-what.

But it always leads to the gargoyle eventually. In her imagination it's either swimming up the river trying to find her, or it's holding a Ping-Pong paddle and staring her down with those glowing green eyes. She's trying to distract herself so she can forget about the gargoyle and just go to bed without looking.

It isn't working.

She sighs and gets up, crosses to the window. She places her fingertips on the cool glass and allows her forehead to touch it as well, looking along the ledge that runs below her window. And there it is: Crouched in his usual place, the muscle-bound wolf/toad/sloth/weasel looks out over the city.

"Good night, yucky thing," she mutters under her breath.

Emma crosses to the bed, pulls back the covers, climbs in, and gets everything just the way she likes it. She turns away from the window and looks at her room. It's a nice room, although dark this time of the night. She can see in the dim light that she needs to clean her room very soon. It's getting hard to walk between the bed and the window. The piles of clothes on the floor look like little creatures that wouldn't put up much of a fight if you-know-who got in.

She closes her eyes, pulls in a big breath to calm herself down, and lets the air out.

And that's when she hears it.

Thump.

"Janie?" Emma whispers. There's no reply. "I'm telling Mom and Dad you're out of bed," she whispers.

Again, no reply, unless you include the new sound she hears. A sound like a nail being dragged slowly down a window.

Scriiiiiiiiiitch.

Emma peers over the covers at the door to her room. It's open about a foot and a half, enough to see that the hallway is pitch black. She turns and looks toward the window. She can't help herself: She slips out of bed and crosses the room.

She has to take one more look.

She has to be sure.

She places her hands against the glass and moves close so she can look along the ledge outside her window, to the right. What did she expect? He's right there.

Back in bed, she reaches for her MP3 player and starts untangling the cord for the earbuds.

Before she can get them in her ears, another noise.

It's a heavy noise.

A lumbering sort of *big* noise.

Shlump.

She puts down the player and stares at the door. "You are *so* grounded," she warns. "I'm telling Mom. She'll be mad."

No response.

She exhales and slouches down in the bed in a pout.

"Stupid statue," she says to herself.

Then: "Stupid me."

She throws back the covers and goes to the window once more, leaning close so she can see down the ledge to the right.

She thinks she's seeing things, having a hallucination or a dream.

Emma rubs her eyes, blinks them four or five times fast, and looks again.

And she gasps.

There's the city.

There's the corner of the ledge.

But there's no gargoyle.

She practically flies into her bed and under the covers.

Thump. Scriiiiiitch.

She peeks over the covers, looking at the black rect-angle that is supposed to be the hallway, the exit, the path to the rest of her family. The path to still being alive when this terrible night comes to an end.

Right then it seems like it's a place she'll never go, a boundary she'll never cross, ever again. It's so far and it's so dark and . . .

Shlump.

She squints into the darkness, trying to see if she can make out a shape. There's a soft, raspy sound. *What is that, breathing?*

Then she notices: In the forbidding blackness, the gloom of the hallway outside her bedroom door, are two heavy-lidded eyes, staring right back at her.

WATCH THE ENDING IF YOU DARE!

Episode 07

A **3:15** Original Story

THE
BEAST

FOR AN AUDIO INTRODUCTION TO THIS
STORY, VISIT WWW.315STORIES.COM

PASSWORD: EVENINGSTAR

t all started with the local newspaper, which had recently been in the habit of overdramatizing the day's events in an effort to hold the attention of a dwindling subscriber base. The *Evening Star* arrived on front porches at "around four P.M." every afternoon. Some of its more exaggerated headlines included MONSOON (an inch of rain and some standing water on the high school baseball field); FIVE-CAR PILEUP (a fender bender in which three of the five cars were vehicles that had only stopped to look); and TOWN BEING OVERRUN BY VAGRANTS (a skateboarding sticker on a downtown lamppost). Soon the locals began looking forward to the next catastrophe, purely for the laugh it provided after a long day of work.

And really, that's the problem with magnifying stories into something bigger than they really are.

Pretty soon, no one takes you seriously. And like bad magic, the universe seems to know precisely when all credibility is lost. That's when you get a headline like the one that ran on a certain Monday, a headline that no one in their right mind was about to believe:

It was, by all accounts, the story that broke the camel's back. People did not believe any part of the headline. Not the idea that a cougar, a beast that hadn't been seen in those parts for years, had even the smallest chance of actually prowling around town. And Wildwood Park? *Please.* Wildwood was in the middle of town, surrounded by houses. It had a baseball field and a walking path, beautiful big trees and a soccer field. It was no place for a giant cat. But the real kicker was the alleged size of the cougar. Three hundred pounds? That, above all other claims, was simply ridiculous.

"What if this thing is real? Should I get a BB gun? I could carry it around with me when I walk the dog."

This is the other big problem with a headline that indicates a 300-pound cougar is menacing the local park. Parents can laugh all they want, but kids believe headlines. At ten years old, Steven sure did. He bought the story hook, line, and sinker.

"Son," said Steven's dad, who had settled in with the crossword puzzle as Steven read from the front page,

"I don't think a BB gun is going to help if you run across a cat the size of a refrigerator."

"What about a baseball bat?" asked Steven. "Or a steak knife?"

Steven's dad wasn't quite sure how to respond. He set his crossword aside and looked at the dog, which needed to be walked.

"This isn't a ploy to get out of your chore, is it?"

"Dad, there's a three-hundred-pound monster in the park," Steven said. "With paws the size of dinner plates. See, it says so, right there."

Steven held out the paper and showed his dad. Chance, the dog in question, stared at Steven's dad in that way he'd come to know all too well.

If you don't take me for a walk now, Chance was saying with those big brown eyes, *I'll wake you up so I can go out in the backyard and pee at two A.M., three A.M., and four A.M. Take your pick.*

And so it was that Steven's dad took Steven and Chance for a walk around Wildwood Park. It was dusk, a chill was in the fall air, and the light was vanishing fast.

"You know," Steven's dad said, "if you can't do this chore on your own, I can't pay you any allowance. That's how it works. You walk the dog every day after school, and I pay you a buck. What are you going to do without five bucks a week?"

It was a reasonable question for a kid with a serious sweet tooth, and with two health nuts for parents. They kept no candy in the house, but every Saturday, Steven was allowed to ride his bike downtown and spend his money on whatever he wanted. There was a candy store on Main Street with jelly beans in about a hundred different flavors. Steven came home on Saturdays with a white paper bag full of the stuff, and it usually lasted him until Sunday at about noon.

"I wonder if a three-hundred-pound cougar would like candy," said Steven. He was holding his baseball bat, which he'd brought along just in case.

They'd reached the far side of the park, where a creek ran along the edge of the path. It was the wildest place in Wildwood; the parks department hadn't bothered to clear the old brush and gnarled, fallen trees.

"I bet it's in there, watching us," said Steven.

"You're worse than the paper," Steven's dad responded, letting Chance off his leash so the dog could run down to the water. "I'm telling you, there's no cougar out here. Did you even read the article?"

"Sure I did. Mrs. Littky, who owns a house right across the street from the park, saw a giant cat lurking around the trees. And you know what's worse than that?" Steven looked at his watch. "It was right about this time. Right when it got dark."

"You do realize Mrs. Littky is practically blind. She's eighty-six."

"She wears glasses," said Steven.

Steven's dad gave up after that. He made a mental note to call the paper and tell them to stop printing overblown headlines. Chance came running back from the water's edge and darted between them, scaring Steven half to death, but that was the only moderately frightening thing that happened on the walk around Wildwood Park.

Steven had to admit it had been awfully quiet. And it was true Mrs. Littky probably couldn't see very well.

The week passed, during which Steven steadfastly forgot to walk the dog after school. There were video games to be played, books that needed reading, homework to do, TV to watch. Not once all week did he remember to walk Chance, and not once would he do it alone after his dad got home. This resulted in a Saturday with no money, and a forty-five-minute begging session that miraculously ended in an advance on his allowance. It was an advance that came with strings attached: There would be no more help from Dad. Starting immediately, Chance was getting walked every day by Steven, alone, no matter what.

But it didn't take very long for Steven to forget about walking the dog. In fact, on that very Saturday, he got very busy. First there was the ride downtown to get the jelly beans. And then there was an afternoon Wiffle ball game in the park. Then his best friend invited him to a movie that turned out to be kind of long. When Steven's dad picked them up, the sun was already setting in the distance.

"Long day, huh?" Steven's dad asked.

"You know it!" said Steven, and then he reeled off all the details of the bike ride, the ball game, the movie.

"Getting a little dark out," Steven's dad said. He'd long since concluded, like all the other adults in town, that there definitely was no 300-pound cougar. If anything was out there, it was more likely an extra-furry house cat wandering beyond the boundaries of its yard. But Steven had stopped paying attention to his dad and instead started talking about a video game with his pal in the backseat. When the friend was dropped off and Steven moved up to the front, Steven's dad turned the headlights on.

"You know, in the autumn, it gets dark kind of early," he explained.

"Yeah, I know, Dad. I'm *ten*."

"Right, you're ten," Steven's dad mumbled. "How's your five bucks holding out?"

"Ummmm . . . fine. I mean, I spent it like usual. I got jelly beans."

"So there's no hope of a refund?"

"Not unless you take jelly beans," answered Steven. "Why would you want a refund?"

And then, like a brick dropped on his foot, Steven understood what his dad was getting at. He looked out the window at the gathering night and gasped.

"I forgot to walk Chance!"

"Yeah, you forgot."

"Can I walk him twice tomorrow? I'll totally do that. I'd even walk him three times. It's Sunday. I'll have time."

"You had time today and the dog didn't get walked *once*. Somehow I doubt he'd get walked twice tomorrow."

Steven didn't have a leg to stand on and he knew it. He'd been shirking his dog-walking duties for over a week, and he'd blown the money on candy. As they pulled into the driveway, it was practically dark. Steven got out of the car and felt a light wind in his face.

"The longer you wait, the darker it's going to get," Steven's dad said. "Better get on with it."

"But, Dad," Steven pleaded. "The three-hundred-pound cougar in the park. The *beast*. What about that?"

They'd been through the park every night for a week and hadn't seen or heard a thing. Even the paper had retracted the story after a second interview with Mrs. Littky in which she stated, "It might have been a possum. But if it was, it was a mighty big one."

Steven followed his dad into the house and put his coat on, then he stuffed the white paper bag of jelly beans in one jacket pocket and a flashlight in the other. He leashed Chance and felt the dog pulling him toward the door.

"You sure you don't want to come with us?" Steven called to his dad on the couch. "Beautiful night out. And I brought snacks."

Steven pulled out the bag of jelly beans, but his dad didn't budge.

"I think I'll pass," said Steven's dad.

Chance pulled Steven through the neighborhood to the gate set in a tall chain-link fence. The fence, which separated Wildwood Park from the surrounding yards, was a comfort, however small. Should he encounter the beast, there was a chance he could run back, lock the monster in, and make it home alive.

Steven chewed a popcorn-flavored jelly bean nervously, unlatched the metal gate, and passed through.

He was in Wildwood Park after dark. Was that even legal? It crossed his mind to tromp right back to his house and ask his dad just that. But he was on thin ice as it was, and if this walk didn't go as planned, it would be even later when he returned to finish the job.

Steven took out his flashlight and turned it on, pointing the beam onto the path. And then he began walking. Well, being pulled, really. Chance was not a huge dog, but he was strong. It was very annoying, being pulled that way. Steven wanted to stay near the tall fence line, but Chance was more interested in smelling everything in the park. Where the dog really wanted to go was down by the water.

"Forget it," said Steven. "We're not going that far. We're staying right here, next to this fence."

But then Steven had an unfortunate thought. If there *was* a beast in the park, and it *did* find him, being against a fence might not be the smartest idea. Having his back to a barrier wouldn't exactly allow for a quick getaway. As Steven considered this problem, Chance caught the scent of a duck or a squirrel or some other park creature and pulled hard and fast, jerking the leash out of Steven's hand.

The dog disappeared into the darkness. As Steven called Chance's name, he quickly realized that it was even scarier in the dark without a dog than it had been *with* one.

Steven ventured a few steps away from the fence, whispering to himself: "There is no beast. There is no beast. Mrs. Littky is mostly blind. I will never forget to walk Chance during the day again. . . ."

His quiet rambling ceased as he neared the water's edge and heard a sound. Peering into the dense thicket, he whispered for the dog.

"Chance? Come on, walk's over."

He stepped cautiously along the path that bordered the creek, continuing to call Chance's name.

He thought he heard another noise — something big trying to step softly and remain unseen as it moved in the dark. He felt his blood run cold and began walking faster, away from the water.

And then he heard it.

A purring — or worse, a low growl.

The beast had found him.

On their first day of kindergarten, Jake, Zach, and Alberto discovered that they shared the same birthday, April fifteenth—also the birthday of Leonardo da Vinci. The boys were inseparable from that point on . . . which is probably why they didn't realize just how unusual they were. They spent most of their time together, just the three of them, all through their childhood and into middle school. And if they noticed in that time that they were more intelligent than those around them, they didn't think too much of it. They simply assumed that if there were three brains like theirs in a small town like Athena, Oregon, then surely there must be a lot more out there somewhere.

But there weren't.

In 1978, Jake, Zach, and Alberto really were the three smartest boys on earth.

People in Athena got used to seeing the threesome huddled together, poring over math textbooks or drafting ideas for new inventions (flying cars were high on their "must create" list). Sometimes, Zach's mom joked that a mysterious force had brought the boys together, what with the shared birthday and the big brains and all.

It was their Saturday night routine that made life in Athena almost perfect for Jake, Zach, and Alberto. Each week, they'd get together at one of their houses for pizza and a *Star Trek* rerun. They'd play video games, read comics, solve complex math problems, and argue about the latest UFO sightings. Sometimes they'd even haul out Zach's telescope and scan the night sky — or just keep an eye on Mount Rainier, which loomed like a ghost on the horizon. The stratovolcano had been the site, in 1948, of one of the most famous UFO sightings of all time.

They called their weekly ritual Nerd Night.

The seventh Nerd Night of 1978 started out during a freak winter thunderstorm. Jagged bolts of lightning ripped across the evening sky. Jake and Alberto showed up at Zach's house right as his parents were rushing out the front door, already late for their bowling league.

"I just ordered the pizza," Zach's mom hollered over her shoulder. "It should be here in forty-five minutes or so. If you need us, call the bowling alley."

When the door slammed closed behind the boys, Nerd Night had officially begun.

"Up here!" Zach hollered from the top of the stairs.

Jake and Alberto knew the drill. They dropped their coats in a pile on the floor and darted up the stairs, following Zach into his bedroom.

Alberto flopped down onto a beanbag chair and started complaining almost immediately. "How come your mom waited so long to order the pizza? I'm starving. . . ."

"You're always starving," Zach said, which was true enough.

"That's because Alberto doesn't realize he has a parasitic alien twin living inside his body," said Jake. "In order for the twin to finish its plans for world conquest, it needs fuel . . . as in cheese, pepperoni, and more cheese."

"That's the dumbest thing I've ever heard," said Alberto, throwing a comic book in Jake's general direction. It missed and smacked Zach in the face.

"How about Oreos while we wait?" Zach suggested, throwing a pillow back at Alberto, who grabbed it in midair with his teeth and pretended to eat it.

Zach was already scrambling off his bed. "There's only eleven Oreos left, and eleven isn't divisible by three," he said. "Last one there gets the short end of the deal!"

The three friends ran out into the hallway, then pushed and shoved all the way down the stairs. They arrived at the kitchen in a pack—just as a mighty crash of thunder rang out. The floor shook, and the windows rattled, followed almost immediately by a brilliant flash that lit up every window in the kitchen.

"Whoa! That was right overhead," Jake said.

"And weird," said Zach.

"What do you mean, weird?" asked Alberto. "It's a storm. It happens."

"I mean the thunder came first, then the lightning. That's not normal."

All three boys looked at each other. They knew the events were out of order, but they also knew it was impossible.

"Maybe we should go up on the roof," Alberto said. "See if it happens again."

"Yeah," Jake said, rolling his eyes. "And get fried by one hundred million volts of electricity."

"And turned into charcoal by an air temperature of fifty thousand degrees Fahrenheit," added Zach.

Before Jake had a chance to reply, there was another flash outside, then a rolling thunderclap. This time, there was nothing unusual about the sequence, and the boys all shrugged at once. Zach mumbled something about a trick of light and sound — then he nearly jumped when the doorbell rang.

"You guys expecting anybody?" he asked.

"Just pizza," Alberto muttered hopefully, licking his lips.

Zach frowned and glanced at his official Darth Vader watch, which was guaranteed water-resistant to one hundred meters. Pizza *already*? No way. His mom and dad had barely been gone five minutes.

The doorbell rang again.

"Okay, okay, on our way!" Zach yelled.

Zach hurried toward the front door, followed closely by Jake and Alberto. As they passed through the living room, Zach glanced out the front window. Despite the darkness outside, he could see a long, low-slung car idling next to the curb.

Can't be Joey, he thought to himself. Joey Turley was the regular pizza delivery guy on Saturday nights, and he always drove a beat-up, dirt-colored Ford Pinto.

Alberto pushed past Zach so he could reach the door first. No surprise there. He was still hoping for the fastest pizza delivery on record. He jerked open the door, took one look at the person standing there, and stumbled back, pulling Zach in front of him for protection.

"Hey, knock it off," Zach said. And then he noticed the man, too, and his mouth went dry.

"You . . . you aren't Joey," Jake stammered.

The man didn't say anything for a moment. He was dressed in a dark suit that didn't quite fit, a white shirt, and a purple tie. On his feet was a pair of red Chuck Taylor sneakers. His eyes — and most of his face — were hidden behind an upturned collar and mirrored sunglasses, even though it had been dark for over an hour already. And wow—he was *tall*. Whoever this guy was, he had to be pushing seven feet.

He held out a flat cardboard box and said one word:

"Pizza."

The voice was slow and monotone, almost like a robot's.

"No, thank you," Jake said quickly, his voice cracking. "Wrong address."

He reached past Zach and began pushing the door closed.

The man stuck his long arm out, holding the door firmly open.

"Pizza."

Alberto gulped audibly as the man held the pizza box out even farther toward the boys.

"For you," he insisted in the same metallic voice.

"Th-that was fast," Alberto said, reaching his hand out slowly until his fingers touched the white cardboard. "Thank you. We really appreciate it. And you're really tall."

Alberto pulled the box into the house, and the man's arm receded into the darkness.

And that's when it hit Zach: This was a prank. It had to be.

"Is that you in there, Joey? Are you on stilts or what?"

But whoever it was turned and started to leave.

"Okay, whatever," Zach said with a laugh. As far as pranks went, this one was pretty cool. "Wait — how much do we owe you?"

"No . . . charge," the man said over his shoulder. Then he marched down the steps, crossed the lawn, and climbed into the weird car.

"Wacko," Zach said as he watched the car's purple taillights disappear slowly down the street. He closed the door, and after a moment's hesitation, he locked the dead bolt.

Zach joined his two friends in the kitchen. They grabbed plates and sodas, then trooped upstairs to Zach's room. Alberto turned on the TV and adjusted the antenna, and they all settled in for *Star Trek*. They'd seen the episode before, but that didn't matter. It was still great. And the pizza was perfect — exactly how they liked it. The dough was thick and chewy, the tomato sauce was rich and tangy, the cheese was fresh, and the top was loaded with pepperoni.

"I think I'm gonna die," Alberto burped twenty minutes later — then he checked the pizza box for any leftovers. "That had to be the greatest pizza the universe has ever known."

Zach and Jake nodded their agreement. It really had been an amazing pizza.

"And the night's only going to get better from there," Zach said with a grin. He reached under his bed and pulled out the latest game console from Atari: the 2600.

"No way!" Jake howled. "You got it!"

"Sweet!" Alberto yelled. "Why didn't you tell us sooner? We could have been playing instead of watching reruns!"

"I love that episode. And no way did I want you getting pizza grease all over the joysticks. Now, who wants to be my first victim in *Combat*?"

Alberto, Jake, and Zach immersed themselves in *Combat*, battling each other to the death as they talked about the computer programming that must have been used to create such amazing graphics.

"Has to be, like, a billion lines of code," said Zach.

"*Ten* billion," said Jake.

If they'd looked outside at that moment, they would have noticed that the storm had passed and the night sky had cleared. They'd have seen Mount Rainier glimmering faintly in the moonlight. And if they'd looked down at the street, they would have also noticed that the strange pizza deliveryman was back. He was standing motionless next to his dark, low-slung car, its purple taillights glowing brightly.

He was staring up at Zach's room.

"You know," Alberto yawned, "the only reason you keep winning is because you've had more practice."

Zach fought back a yawn of his own. "In your dreams," he said. "Who's next?"

But instead of a smart-aleck retort, Zach heard a different sound. Jake was lying facedown on the floor, snoring.

"What a big baby," Zach said with a shake of his head. He turned his attention to Alberto. "I guess that means it's you and m —"

Alberto was sitting on the floor, leaning up against the bookshelf. His eyes were closed.

Zach rubbed his face, yawned, and then struggled to his feet.

Something weird was going on, but he was so tired, he couldn't quite pin it down. He glanced out the window, and some part of his brain noticed a car with purple tail-lights parked in front of his house.

"What's he doing here?" Zach asked himself. But he was suddenly so tired, he couldn't keep his eyes open any longer. The last thing he saw was the man taking some-thing out of his pocket and pointing it at the house. There was a little purple dot of light, then nothing.

Zach sat down on the floor, curled up into a ball, and fell fast asleep.

And then the pizza box started to move.

WATCH THE ENDING IF YOU DARE!

LOG ON NOW TO SEE THE CHILLING CONCLUSION. . . .

315STORIES.COM
PASSWORD: PEPPERONI

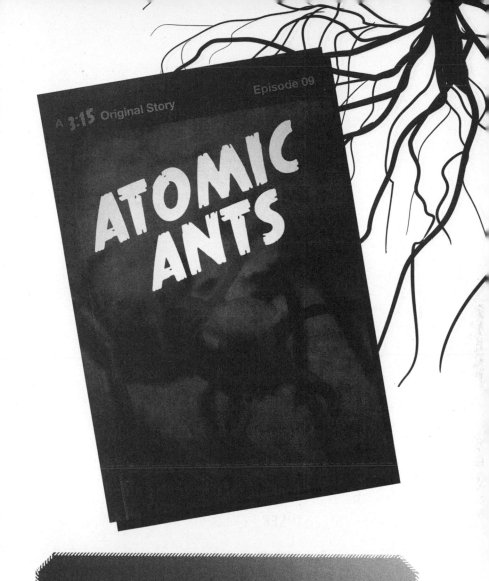

Episode 09

A **3:15** Original Story

ATOMIC ANTS

amp Mead closed down for good after the summer of 1992. There had been a lot of rumors floating around the camp that year, and far too many unanswered questions — most of which had to do with the disappearance of Eddie Lansing. How was it that a teenager had simply vanished off the face of the earth in the middle of the night? And most unusual of all: Why did his cabinmates insist on such an unbelievable story about what had befallen the missing Eddie Lansing?

Twenty years later, an urban legend about what really happened to Eddie endures. Many believe the legend is true, in part because the facts add up. But also because the story has been told around campfires for two decades. A story that stays around that long has to be true, doesn't it?

The tale begins with a commonly agreed-upon fact: Eddie was not well liked. He was a boy who so annoyed the other eighth graders at the camp that they wouldn't have anything to do with him. He was big for his age, overbearing, clumsy, and mean.

And he happened to like picking on smaller, younger kids at Camp Mead. Most of his energy, in fact, was spent tripping, pushing, and otherwise tormenting the fifth graders. It was they who were new to the camp, they who were the smallest and weakest. And of the many fifth graders, a select and terribly unlucky group of four were placed in a cabin overseen by Eddie Lansing himself.

Cabin number two.

That's where these poor souls were sent.

And Eddie Lansing took to his job like a hog to slop.

"Canteen!" he yelled on the very first afternoon of camp. He was lying on his bunk in cabin number two, his arms folded behind his head, while the four helpless fifth graders obeyed his every whim. "You, what's your name again? Rippy?"

"Rudy, sir," said a sunburned little kid with bright blue eyes. "My name is Rudy."

"Right, Rupy, whatever. You and that Pete kid go get me a licorice whip and an orange soda. Pronto."

Rudy, having had his name butchered twice, turned to the group of three boys standing beside him. Pete, a lanky towheaded geek, was already turning toward the door, only too happy for a chance to get away from the cabin.

"I'll go, too!" yelled both of the other boys — Jeff and Anthony — and like a nerd herd, the four boys ran for the door, while Eddie Lansing called for them to come back and fill out a cabin report he had no intention of doing himself. The boys ignored him, none of them brave enough to break from the pack and return alone.

"Bad decision, cabinmates," Eddie said as he closed his eyes and settled in for a nap. "Very bad decision."

The tormenting didn't stop when Pete, Rudy, Jeff, and Anthony returned with the red rope and the orange soda. He made them unpack his suitcase and get his dinner so he wouldn't have to wait in line in the mess hall. During the first two days, they found their beds short-sheeted, and shaving cream in their tennis shoes. And it was horrible at night, when Eddie snored and his feet stank so bad they had to plug their noses.

But there was one activity Eddie liked more than anything else, and it made all the other ways he mistreated the boys seem tame in comparison.

He loved to scare people.

He would hide behind the door and leap out at the young campers as they came into the cabin. He would put bugs and plastic snakes in their beds. And, worst of all, he would tell them stories.

"You know," he said on the third night, as the boys were plugging their noses while Eddie wiggled his stinky toes. "There's a red-faced maniac lives in these woods. He always shows up on the third night looking for one kid. Just one."

"Why does he need a kid?" asked Jeff, his voice trembling.

"No one knows for sure. Rumor says he drags that one kid out into the woods and leaves him for dead."

"Did you lock the cabin door?" asked Anthony.

Eddie got up and pulled the cabin door wide open.

"Better leave it open or it'll get hot in here. Plus, someone's feet stink. You guys are gross."

An hour later, when the fifth graders had finally managed to fall asleep, Eddie grabbed Rudy by the foot and dragged him screaming out of the cabin. He laughed and laughed as kids came flooding out of every door, wondering what all the commotion was about.

Eddie thought it was the funniest thing he'd ever done.

After that, the four boys gave up any hope of defying Eddie. None of them wanted the Red-Faced Maniac treatment, that was for sure. They barely slept, did constant errands and chores, and worried endlessly about what might appear in their shoes, their dinner, or their hair.

On the fifth day of camp, Eddie decided to institute a forced march into the woods. He had a diabolical plan in mind, one he kept to himself as they hiked a mile down an overgrown trail that wound into the mountains. Eventually, they came to a locked gate in a long barbed-wire fence. On the gate was a sign that read:

Keep Out. Private Property.

"Come on," he said, parting the cords of barbed wire so the boys could fit through. "Got something I want to show you. It's cool. You'll dig it."

Rudy and the rest were wary of Eddie, but they kind of wanted to know what lay beyond the fence line, too. So far, camp hadn't been half the adventure they'd hoped for.

They pushed aside their misgivings and stepped forward. Anthony went first, then Jeff and Pete, and finally Rudy.

"Follow me," Eddie said, after clambering through the fence and getting his T-shirt stuck, ripping a hole down the side.

"Maybe we should just go back," Rudy said, feeling less comfortable than he'd thought he might, now that they were on the other side of the fence.

Eddie laughed.

"I always knew you were a chicken, Rupy."

"I'm Rudy, not Rupy."

"Whatever," Eddie said, leading the boys farther still.

They came to a small clearing bordered by five large trees.

"If you look to the sky, it's a star."

The boys looked up, and sure enough, the canopy of trees above outlined the shape of a five-sided star.

"Cool," said Pete. "Can we go back to camp now? I'm hungry."

"Hold your horses. That's not even the best part," said Eddie. "Do you guys know what this place used to be?"

Anthony raised his hand.

"This ain't school," Eddie said, laughing. "You guys are such dweebs. You'll never guess, so I'll just tell you. This whole area used to be a nuclear waste dump."

"No way," said Rudy, staring at his arms like he thought they might start glowing green.

"*Yeah*, way," Eddie said in a serious voice. He took a few steps to his right, knelt down, and started brushing away the pine needles and dirt. Soon he had revealed a round, flat concrete block that sat on the forest floor.

"What is it?" asked Jeff, creeping a little closer.

"It's a lid."

"What's inside?" asked Anthony. All the boys were standing around the edge of the concrete circle.

"Way down there, like a thousand feet down, that's where they put all the metal drums of radioactive waste."

"You're so lying," said Rudy, but he was uneasy just the same.

"And you want to know what else is down there?" asked Eddie.

"Not really," said Pete. The other boys shook their heads in agreement.

"Ants. But not normal ones. *Huge* ants, like six feet long. The Atomic Ants."

None of the boys spoke. It couldn't be true—but somehow, there under the canopy of trees that made the shape of a star over their heads, it seemed like it was possible.

Something moved behind them, a bird or some other small animal in the underbrush, and all four young boys jumped.

Eddie shook his head, thinking: *Dweebs. This is gonna be great.*

"Last year, one of them got out and came into camp," Eddie said. "Tried to drag some kid away. They say it was huge, with wicked sharp pincers."

Eddie was in full swing now, really going for it.

"They had to beat it back with a shovel. Took seven guys to kill it."

"How did it get out? I mean, they're trapped down there, right?"

"Someone removed the lid," Eddie said, and then he leaned down low and placed his hands on the edge of the round concrete slab. He pushed, putting his whole back into it, sliding the lid away with a horrible grinding noise.

"What are you doing?" yelled Rudy. "Put it back! Are you crazy?!"

But Eddie kept pushing until the slab was three-quarters of the way off, leaving a hole big enough to fall through. He leaned down, putting his head in the hole, and called to whatever was down there.

"Helllloooooooooo! Come out, come out, wherever you are!"

And then he laughed and laughed and started walking back in the direction from which they'd come. All four boys tried desperately to push the concrete lid back on, but no matter how hard they tried, they couldn't do it.

All four of them put together weren't as strong as Eddie Lansing. They chased after their cabin leader and begged him to put the lid back in place, but Eddie told them he couldn't do it.

"You better stay up all night, I guess, just in case," he said. "Chances are, whatever comes out of that hole, it'll be looking for one of you."

The rest of the hike was long and quiet as the young campers whispered among themselves about finding a shovel and taking shifts staying awake.

Eddie was beaming with satisfaction at the trick he'd played.

If only he had known that he was right about the radioactive waste site.

If only Eddie Lansing hadn't pushed the lid off the containment unit.

Maybe Camp Mead would still be open today.

But it's not.

Because late that very night, in the quiet of a moonlit summer camp, whatever had been down in that hole crept silently closer.

And whatever crawled outside the window of cabin number two was hungry.

WATCH THE ENDING IF YOU DARE!

A **3:15** Original Story

Episode 10

NIGHT ON THE DREDGE

FOR AN AUDIO INTRODUCTION TO THIS
STORY, VISIT WWW.315STORIES.COM

PASSWORD: APOSTLE

keleton Creek has recently drifted back into the quiet place it once was. I had come to expect a certain upward momentum, an ever-increasing buzz of excitement in my tiny mountain town. But that wasn't meant to last. Skeleton Creek is starting to feel like the same deathly boring place it was before it got interesting for about ten whole seconds. What I wouldn't give for some of that old Skeleton Creek magic to return, even for a few days. The ghostly nights. The crazy adventures. And Sarah.

Mostly it's about Sarah.

She's been gone a long time now, but I miss her just the same.

It was this combination of boredom and loneliness that led to what I found.

Apparently I'm never going to learn that digging around in Skeleton Creek's past always leads to the same thing: trouble.

First, in case someone reading this has no idea what I'm talking about, a quick primer:

- My name is Ryan McCray and I live in a small town called Skeleton Creek. (I hope you picked up on that much, at least.)

- A lot of bad things happened here in the past, most of it centered around the old dredge in the woods outside of town. Some people believe it's haunted. I'm one of them.

- I'm part of a secret society called the Crossbones. There are only three of us: Fitz, Sarah Fincher, and me. We don't really know what our job is because we're new at it, but we're figuring it out. Before us, there were three others who made up the Crossbones: the Raven (also Fitz's dad), Henry, and the Apostle.

- Henry and the Apostle are dead; only the Raven is still alive. Some people say the Raven lives deep in the woods and goes by many names, one of them Chandler. He's said to know many stories. I think we'd get along. But the Raven, or Chandler, whatever he calls himself, is a recluse. He never leaves the woods.

- The ghost of Old Joe Bush is a complicated matter, but all you need to know is this: The ghost has never left the dredge. It haunts the dredge for many reasons, and it will never stop.
- It was the Apostle's job to keep the records for the Crossbones before I got involved. The Raven, Henry, and the Apostle were a shadowy bunch with a lot of secrets, some of which I helped bring to light. And they didn't like each other.

The questions I started asking myself in the gathering quiet of Skeleton Creek were these:

What really happened on the night when the Apostle died?

Where did he live?

Were there any clues about him I might have missed along the way?

It turns out I did miss some things.

Big, weird, scary things.

Here's what I found, exactly as I remember it.

"How many times have I told you to leave the past well enough alone?"

Gladys Morgan, the town librarian, was staring down her nose at me, her glasses looking as if they might slide right off her wrinkled face.

"You're the dumbest kid I ever met."

"I'm not dumb, Gladys," I said. "I'm curious."

"Same difference."

"Just tell me where he lived," I asked for the third time. "I just want to look at his house. What's the big deal?"

"The dead don't like it when you put an ax to their stuff."

Miss Morgan was still sore about the fact that I'd recently been involved in the ripping up of her library floor. Long story, not a pretty sight.

"I just want to look at it, that's all," I said.

She pointed to the door without another word, and I knew all hope was lost. She'd sooner smile at me than give me a shred of information about the Apostle. And she was never, ever going to smile at me.

Other results were similar.

I tried the church where the Apostle used to attend. Result: a big zero.

I tried the old guys at the fly fishing club. Result: an uncomfortable silence.

I tried my dad. Result: "Go ask Gladys Morgan." (Not helpful.)

I had almost given up on the idea of ever discovering where the Apostle had lived so many years ago, but I decided there was one place that might hold an answer or two: the dredge, which still sat in the woods outside Skeleton Creek. I wouldn't go in there at night — not anymore — but during the day, it only scared me *half* to death, not all the way dead.

It had been months since I'd been out there. In that time they'd fixed up the path and started offering daily tours at ten A.M. with all sorts of facts about the dredge, the gold that was found there, and the history of mining. Kind of boring stuff, actually, but it didn't make it any less nerve-racking.

The dredge was just as huge and desolate as I

remembered. It felt haunted even in the late afternoon light. I passed through the giant doors and looked up at the rusted-out gears and conveyer belts. Something moved along the floor — a mouse or a rat — and I yelled, hearing my own voice echo into the great open space above my head.

"You can do this, Ryan, just calm down."

There was one place where I might find facts of some use. Gathering my courage, I started in that direction, up a rickety switchback stairway, steep and rotting. At the top, a chain barred the way, with a sign: No ADMITTANCE. STAFF ONLY.

Maybe some kid had tried to peel away from the tour and climb up here, so they'd had to install the sign. It didn't really matter. What I needed to find was beyond the chain, so I carefully climbed over and kept going. The steps led to a narrow hall, with windows on one side, that ended in another set of stairs that took me higher still. The gears from up here — despite being massive — looked like they were floating in the air.

When I reached the control room for the dredge,

I found the door locked. The funny thing was, a thin glass window next to the locked door had been almost completely knocked out. I put my arm through, unlocked the door, and entered.

Inside were levers and controls, wires and pulleys, all sorts of ancient mechanisms for controlling the dredge. But I also knew this was the room that had acted as the office for the dredge. There was a bank of wooden drawers on the wall, none of them very big, and I started pulling them out one by one. A lot of the drawers held data cards, like an old card catalogue at a library, each card reporting how much gold was logged on a given day. Other drawers held maps of the area, routes the dredge would take, power supply information. Mostly boring stuff, until I came to the drawer I was looking for: employee records.

Back when the dredge was running, it had been a major employer in town. Aside from those who worked on the dredge itself, many people worked sorting and weighing the gold, or doing restoration work where the dredge had been, or providing repairs, or any number of other things that go along with a major mining operation.

The cards were in alphabetical order, and I knew the Apostle's real name: Bill Hampstead. As I flipped through the deck, my hands were shaking. The wind was blowing outside, which made the dredge rock in the water it sat on as I came to the Apostle's card.

William Hampstead
Accounting clerk
Nonsalaried contract
Status: dismissed, disruptive conduct
Address: Last known — Rm. 302, Mills Hotel, Local

Despite crabby old Gladys Morgan, I'd found what I was looking for: a possible window into the past.

I turned to go and, doing so, found that I wasn't alone.

A huge feral cat stared up at me from the doorway like it owned the place. This is one of the reasons I do not like cats: They're stealthy as all get-out. This thing had probably followed me all the way through the dredge without me knowing about it, and now it was barring my escape as if it wouldn't let me leave if I didn't feed it.

I moved in its direction and it hissed at me.

Then I heard a different noise, like the sound of a man dragging his broken leg behind him. It was the signature sound of the ghost of the dredge—a sound I knew all too well.

"Cat, if you don't move, I'll have to punt you into next week."

Was it my imagination or did the cat take a step closer?

And was I hearing the ghost of the dredge or was I just in one of my ultra-imaginative moments?

I lunged for the cat and it crouched lower. It was thirty pounds of claws and matted fur, and it was mad.

How do I get myself into these situations?

I heard the dragging leg again, closer now, and decided I'd rather risk the cat than the ghost. I ran for the door, jumped over the stray animal, and felt it reaching up to grab my legs. Its claws caught on my pants. I dragged the cat a foot or two, then it let loose and I was running through the long corridors, down the treacherous stairs, and out into the light of day.

I took only one look back and saw the cat staring at me from a window far above. The dredge sat in silence on the water, daring me to come back inside. But I didn't need to.

I'd found what I was looking for.

Three hours later I knew a bit more. The Mills Hotel was never really what you could technically call a hotel at all. It was more a boardinghouse, which had since been transformed into a private residence. What I could glean on my own searching through historical records:

- There had been six rooms divided among three stories.
- The hotel had been run by a couple, now deceased.
- It had been sold four times in the intervening years, landing in the hands of one Drew Mobley a scant six months previous.
- It was within short walking distance of my house.

The Apostle's residence had been right under my nose all these years, which I found both astonishing and expected. Skeleton Creek was home to many secrets, most of them just below the surface. And I did not, generally speaking, live in a town of curious folks. People in Skeleton Creek were perfectly happy to leave the past where it was, just like Gladys Morgan.

I looked down the street from my front steps and found that the sun was setting. Twilight had come to Skeleton Creek as I started my short journey to the Mills Hotel. When I stood before it, I wouldn't have guessed that it had ever been a hotel or even a boardinghouse. It was a standard three-story house, not terribly big, with an unkempt lawn. There were toys scattered on the front porch, so it didn't surprise me when a child answered the door.

"Are your parents home?" I asked, staring down at a dark-haired boy of six or seven.

"Dad!" the kid yelled over his shoulder, and then he was gone, like he had something much more important to do.

When the dad arrived at the door, I put on my best face.

"Mr. Mobley, right?"

"Yeah," he said, amiable as could be. "And you're Ryan McCray. Nice to finally meet you."

He put his hand out and I shook it. I'd enjoyed some moments of renown in Skeleton Creek having to do with hidden treasures, and I got the feeling Mr. Mobley was new enough in town that I could use this to my advantage. We chatted on the front porch until I got around to mentioning the hotel.

"Really?" he asked. "No one ever mentioned that about the place. Must have been a long time ago."

"It was," I said, then made my move. "Listen, Mr. Mobley, I'm researching a certain aspect of the town's past that involves a resident who stayed here for a while. Would there be any chance of me taking a look in his old room?"

"I don't see why not," he said, stepping inside and ushering me in behind him. "Who knows? Maybe there's something valuable in here, right?"

"Could be," I said, watching the door close behind me. "It was room 302, so I'm guessing that's the top floor."

He started up the stairs.

"You'll have to excuse the mess up there. We haven't had time to remodel and it's definitely in need of a face-lift. Luke!"

The little kid was back, walking up the stairs at my heels.

"Tell your mother I'm going upstairs, will you, buddy? I'll be down in a few."

The boy ran back down the stairs two at a time as we arrived on the third floor.

"That one's Luke's room. It's standard issue toy land in there. But this one . . ." He opened another door on the opposite side of the hallway. "This one hasn't had much done to it in a while. I was thinking of using it as a study eventually. Any idea what you're looking for?"

I shook my head as I entered the room, suddenly feeling spooked by the whole idea of being in the same place the Apostle had been.

The room had been redone once or twice over the years, maybe more, but it still felt old and neglected.

"Dad! Dinner!" Luke yelled from the bottom of the stairs. The kid was a real screamer.

"Hang on a sec, be right there," Mr. Mobley yelled back. He looked at me, sort of sizing me up, I guess, then shrugged. "I gotta get downstairs or she'll flip out. Stop by the table on the way out; stay for dinner if you like."

"Thanks, Mr. Mobley — I already ate, but this is great. I'll just look around is all."

When Mr. Mobley was gone, I got right down to business. The Apostle had been the record keeper for the Crossbones, and he'd kept a lot of dirt on the other members. It was this dirt that had gotten him in trouble with Henry, one of the other members of the Crossbones. Henry was dead, but the secrets, I was sure, remained.

And I had a feeling they were in this room.

But where?

The Apostle had been in the habit of filming himself with an old reel-to-reel camera. He'd kept the film reels in small canisters and hid them all over the place. If there was another reel, one we'd never found, where would it be?

I searched for a full five minutes and found nothing. The room was all bare walls and restored floor, nothing much to find. There wasn't even a closet — and that got me thinking: This probably wouldn't have been a room someone stayed in. It was too small, too basic.

I went out in the hall, scanned the doors, and thought: *It's the kid's room. That's where the Apostle stayed. That was room 302 of the Mills Hotel.*

I heard voices downstairs as I put my hand on the door handle and turned. The door felt like it might be the original, hardwood and painted over a bunch of times. It opened with a low creak.

The room was a mess of clothes and toys. A bed rested against the far wall, and a dresser sat to my left, on top of which was a cage with a lizard inside. It was staring at me.

"Oh, brother," I said. "I'll never find anything in here."

I did a quick search of the corners in the room, the closet, the air vent, and found nothing. I looked in every direction, my eyes landing on the door again.

That old, old door.

As a last-ditch effort I grabbed a red plastic table and moved it close to the door, then stood on top of it. Feeling along the length of the top of the door, I discovered a tiny ridge.

Bingo! I thought, and went in search of something I could use to pry a wood plug out of a door. What I needed was a flat-blade screwdriver and a hammer, but all I could come up with was a dirty spoon and a shoe. The spoon would be my wedge, the shoe my hammer. It was the best I was going to get.

"Whatcha doin' in my room?"

The voice came from the doorway behind me, and it made me jump back toward the dresser. I turned, feeling more than a little awkward. I had this kid's shoe in one hand and a spoon in the other.

"Cool room, little dude," I said, looking at the shoe. "And this is a great shoe. I mean really, just a great shoe."

"Dad says you should come down and say hi to my mom. She wants to meet you."

"Perfect! I'd love to. And I have a spoon, so I can eat."

"Gross," Luke said, crinkling up his face. "I use that spoon to clean out Melvin's cage." Luke motioned to the lizard on top of the dresser. "It's my poop scoop."

Lovely.

Luke laughed and started down the stairs, yelling to his dad about the spoon, and I bolted back to the door. I had maybe a minute more, that was it.

From the top of the plastic table, I could just see the upper edge of the door. The wooden plug was about an inch wide and six inches long, and it was really jammed in there. I rapped the spoon with the shoe, digging into one corner, then wobbled the spoon back and forth. Repeating that routine on all four sides resulted in a popping sound as the wooden plug came loose.

"Ryan? You okay up there?" Mr. Mobley called from the bottom of the stairs.

"Yeah, great—just coming down!"

I removed the plug and reached into the hole it had sealed.

My fingers touched something inside, but I couldn't get a hold of whatever it was.

Think fast, Ryan. You have, like, ten seconds! I thought.

I looked at the spoon, flipped it over to hold it by its gross scooping end, and wedged the thin metal handle down against the edge of the opening. Then I flicked my wrist and a small, round film canister popped out, flew through the air, and landed on top of the lizard cage.

I barely had time to drop the spoon and the shoe and pocket the film reel before Mr. Mobley appeared in the doorway.

"I-I got to thinking, this was probably the room," I stammered. "But it's pretty messy in here, not much point in trying to find clues from the past."

"Yeah, I figured as much," said Mr. Mobley, looking around the room as well, his eyes finally settling on me. "The only ancient thing you'll find in here is Luke's dirty socks."

We both laughed, and as we left the room, I realized I'd put the rectangular wooden plug in my back pocket.

And in the other pocket, a reel of film that would give me nightmares for months.

It took me a while to find a projector that would play the reel of film I'd found. My friend Sarah had one, but she was all the way across the country. And she wouldn't have let me borrow it, anyway. Between finding one online, bidding for it over a period of days, and getting it shipped to my house, I couldn't do anything more than stare at that reel of film for two whole weeks.

When the projector finally did arrive, I set it up in my room and pointed it at the wall. The thing about these old projectors, it has to be dark in order for them to work very well, so I had to watch the film at night with the lights turned off.

What I found was a series of videos that gave me three pieces of information:

- The Apostle had known who I was . . . and I hadn't even been born yet. Creepy.
- The Apostle had been murdered.
- The dredge isn't only haunted now. It'd been haunted then, too.

I had the footage converted to video.

I gave the video, along with this story, to the Raven, the last surviving Crossbones member.

I don't want anything more to do with it.

WATCH THE ENDING IF YOU DARE!

LOG ON NOW TO SEE THE CHILLING CONCLUSION. . . .

315STORIES.COM
PASSWORD: MILLSHOTEL

Paul Chandler

lives in the woods outside of the town of ████████████████████████, Linkford. As a long-time member of ████████████████████████ ████████████████ Mr. Chandler is no stranger to secrets. He's begun to collect them in the form of stories.

To learn more about the author, ████████████████████████████ ████████████████████████████

Credits

STORY CONCEPTS, WRITING, AND EDITING
Patrick Carman
with contributions by
Michael Wenberg
Jeffrey Townsend
Matthew McKern
Nicholas Eliopulos

VIDEOS
Mechan Media
ZF Creative
Jeffrey Townsend
Daniel FitzSimmons

AUDIO FILES
Now What Creative

WEB AND APP DEVELOPMENT
Joshua Pease
Brian Griffiths
Christa Mowry

ART AND ALTERNATE REALITY ELEMENTS
Joshua Pease

With special thanks to David Levithan, Peter
Rubie, and Susan Schulman for stepping out on
the ledge once more.

THERE WAS A MOMENT NOT LONG AGO WHEN I THOUGHT: <u>THIS IS IT. I'M DEAD.</u>

I THINK ABOUT THAT NIGHT ALL THE TIME AND I FEEL THE SAME FEAR I FELT THEN. IT HAPPENED TWO WEEKS AGO, BUT FOURTEEN DAYS AND NIGHTS OF REMEMBERING HAVE LEFT ME MORE AFRAID AND UNCERTAIN THAN EVER.

WHICH I GUESS MEANS IT ISN'T OVER YET. SOMETHING TELLS ME IT MAY NEVER TRULY BE OVER.

LAST NIGHT WAS THE FIRST TIME I SLEPT IN MY OWN ROOM SINCE EVERYTHING HAPPENED. I'D GOTTEN IN THE HABIT OF WAKING IN THE HOSPITAL TO THE SOUND OF A NURSE'S SHUFFLING FEET, THE DRY CHALK-DUST SMELL OF HER SKIN, AND THE SOFT SHAKING OF MY SHOULDER.

<u>THE DOCTOR WILL VISIT YOU IN A MOMENT. HE'LL WANT YOU AWAKE. CAN YOU SIT UP FOR ME, RYAN?</u>

THERE WAS NO NURSE OR DOCTOR OR CHALKY SMELL THIS MORNING, ONLY THE EARLY TRAIN CRAWLING THROUGH TOWN TO WAKE ME AT HALF PAST FIVE. BUT IN MY WAKING MIND, IT WASN'T A TRAIN I HEARD. IT WAS SOMETHING MORE MENACING, TRYING TO SNEAK PAST IN THE EARLY DAWN, GLANCING DOWN THE DEAD-END STREETS, HUNTING.

I WAS SCARED — AND THEN I WAS RELIEVED — BECAUSE MY OVERACTIVE IMAGINATION HAD SETTLED BACK INTO ITS NATURAL RESTING STATE OF FEAR AND PARANOIA.

IN OTHER WORDS, I WAS BACK HOME IN SKELETON CREEK.

USUALLY WHEN THE MORNING TRAIN WAKES ME UP, I GO STRAIGHT TO MY DESK AND START WRITING BEFORE THE REST OF THE TOWN STARTS TO STIR. BUT THIS MORNING — AFTER SHAKING THE IDEA THAT SOMETHING WAS STALKING ME — I HAD A SUDDEN URGE TO LEAP FROM MY BED AND JUMP ON BOARD THE TRAIN. IT WAS A FEELING I DIDN'T EXPECT AND HADN'T THE SLIGHTEST CHANCE OF ACTING ON. BUT STILL, I WONDERED WHERE THE FEELING HAD COME FROM.

NOW, I'VE RESTED THIS JOURNAL ON A TV TRAY WITH ITS LEGS TORN OFF, PROPPED MYSELF UP IN BED ON A COUPLE OF PILLOWS, AND HAVE STARTED DOING THE ONE THING I CAN STILL DO THAT HAS ALWAYS MADE ME FEEL BETTER.

I HAVE BEGUN TO WRITE ABOUT THAT NIGHT AND ALL THAT COMES AFTER.

I need to take breaks. It still hurts to write. Physically, mentally, emotionally — it seems like every part of me is broken in one way or another. But I have to start doing this again. Two weeks in the hospital without a journal left me starving for words.

I have kept a lot of journals, but this one is especially important for two reasons. Reason number one: I'm not writing this for myself. I'm putting these words down for someone else to find, which is something I never do. Reason number two: I have a strong feeling this will be the last journal I ever write.

My name, in case someone finds this and cares to know who wrote it, is Ryan. I'm almost old enough to drive. (Although this would require access to a car, which I lack.) I'm told that I'm tall for my age but need to gain weight or there's no hope of making the varsity cut next year. I have a great hope that I will remain thin.

I can imagine what this morning would have

BEEN LIKE BEFORE THE ACCIDENT. I WOULD BE GETTING READY FOR THE HOUR-LONG BUS RIDE TO SCHOOL. I WOULD HAVE SO MUCH TO SAY TO SARAH. AN HOUR NEXT TO HER WAS ALWAYS TIME WELL-SPENT. WE HAD SO MUCH IN COMMON, WHICH KEPT US FROM GOING COMPLETELY CRAZY IN A TOWN POPULATED BY JUST UNDER SEVEN HUNDRED PEOPLE.

I'M REALLY GOING TO MISS THOSE CONVERSATIONS WITH SARAH. I WONDER IF I'LL GET LONELY. THE TRUTH IS I DON'T EVEN KNOW IF I'M ALLOWED TO MENTION HER NAME. BUT I CAN'T STOP. I AM A WRITER. THIS IS WHAT I DO. MY TEACHERS, PARENTS, EVEN SARAH — THEY ALL SAY I WRITE TOO MUCH, THAT I'M OBSESSIVE ABOUT IT. BUT THEN, IN THE SAME BREATH, THEY CAN'T HELP BUT MENTION THAT I'M GIFTED. LIKE WHEN MRS. GARVEY TOLD ME I UNDERSTAND WORDS AND THEIR USAGE IN THE SAME WAY A PRODIGY ON THE PIANO UNDERSTANDS NOTES AND SOUNDS. BUT I HAVE A MUCH SIMPLER ANSWER, AND I'M PRETTY SURE I'M MORE RIGHT THAN MY TEACHER IS: I HAVE WRITTEN A LOT, EVERY DAY, EVERY YEAR, FOR MANY YEARS IN A ROW.

PRACTICE MAKES PERFECT.

I THINK MY FAVORITE WRITERS ARE THOSE WHO ADMITTED WHILE THEY WERE STILL ALIVE THAT THEY COULDN'T LIVE WITHOUT WRITING. JOHN STEINBECK, ERNEST HEMINGWAY, ROBERT FROST — GUYS WHO PUT WRITING UP THERE IN THE SAME CATEGORY AS AIR AND WATER. WRITE OR DIE TRYING. THAT KIND OF THINKING AGREES WITH ME.

BECAUSE HERE I AM. WRITE OR DIE TRYING.

IF I TURN BACK THE PAGES IN ALL THE JOURNALS I'VE WRITTEN, I BASICALLY FIND TWO THINGS: SCARY STORIES OF MY OWN CREATION AND THE RECORDING OF STRANGE OCCURRENCES IN SKELETON CREEK. I CAN'T SAY FOR CERTAIN WHY THIS IS SO, OTHER THAN TO FALL BACK ON THE OLD ADAGE THAT A WRITER WRITES WHAT HE KNOWS, AND I HAVE KNOWN FEAR ALL MY LIFE.

I DON'T THINK I'M A COWARD — I WOULDN'T BE IN THE POSITION I'M IN NOW IF I WAS A COWARD — BUT I AM THE SORT OF PERSON WHO OVERANALYZES, WORRIES, FRETS. WHEN I HEAR A NOISE SCRATCHING UNDER THE BED — EITHER REAL OR IMAGINED — I STARE AT THE CEILING FOR HOURS AND WONDER WHAT IT MIGHT BE THAT'S TRYING TO CLAW ITS WAY OUT. (I PICTURE IT WITH FANGS, LONG BONY FINGERS, AND BULGING RED

EYES.) FOR A PERSON WHO WORRIES LIKE I DO AND HAS A VIVID IMAGINATION TO MATCH, SKELETON CREEK IS THE WRONG SORT OF PLACE TO ENDURE CHILDHOOD.

I KNOW MY WRITING HAS CHANGED IN THE PAST YEAR. THE TWO KINDS OF WRITING — THE MADE-UP SCARY STORIES AND THE DOCUMENTING OF EVENTS IN SKELETON CREEK — HAVE SLOWLY BECOME ONE. I DON'T HAVE TO MAKE UP STORIES ANY LONGER, BECAUSE I'M MORE CERTAIN THAN EVER THAT THE VERY TOWN I LIVE IN IS HAUNTED.

THIS IS THE TRUTH.

AND THE TRUTH, I'VE LEARNED, CAN KILL YOU.

I'M TIRED NOW. SO TIRED.

I HAVE TO PUT THIS DOWN.

EVEN IF I CAN'T STOP THINKING ABOUT IT.

SARAHFINCHER.COM
PASSWORD: HOUSEOFUSHER

How far back can you go, Adam?

What do you mean?

I think you know what I mean. Start at the beginning.

The very beginning?

Yes. I need to know everything.

There's no way for you to know everything. We'd be in here for a month.

What I mean is — don't hold anything back. If you think it's relevant, I want to know about it.

Like I have a choice.

Yes, you do. The ball is in your court. You can play this however you like. Just remember, it's not only your future on the line here. This is about a lot more people than you, Adam Henderson.

Subject stared coldly at the two-way mirror, appeared to be weighing his options one last time. He has all the answers stored in his mind, waiting to be downloaded. Everything we need is in there, if only I can get him moving in the right direction.

It began with a guy who went camping all by himself in the 1960s and got lost. I mean, like, *really* lost.

Adam, I don't think we need to go back fifty years. That's not what I meant.

You want the whole story or don't you?

I want the whole story.

Then stop interrupting me.

It was a huge forest, bigger than five counties, full of bears and cougars and rattlers. The forest service sent in this old tracker — a big-bearded, long-haired, cowboy hat–wearing mountain man, the last of his kind. *They don't make 'em like that anymore* — that's what everybody said about this tracker dude. He didn't work for the government or the police or anything like that. He lived deep in the woods and knew its secrets. A real tracker knows his terrain inside and out.

It took him three days of walking in the wild all alone in the cold and the rain to find what he was looking for: a man sitting with his back against a tree, miles from anything resembling a trail, holding nothing but an empty water bottle in one hand and a Buck knife in the other. The tracker looked down and said, and I quote, "Get up off your sorry butt. We got some walking to do."

Believe it or not this guy — the tracker in the story — he wasn't just any mountain man, he was my grandfather. I realize this is hard to believe, given the way I live, but it's the plain truth, and it's important.

I never met Old Henderson, which is what my dad calls my grandfather when he tells me these stories, because Old

Henderson met up with a grizzly one day and never came back. My dad was just a kid, so, as you might imagine, this took the shine off the outdoors. He hated the woods after that, moved to Seattle the first chance he got, and never looked back.

Why are you telling me these things, Adam?

Because my urban existence doesn't change a thing about where I came from. My grandfather was a legendary tracker, in a mud-under-his-fingernails sort of way. And more than that, he had a knack for landing himself in the most dangerous situations. You know how family traits have a way of skipping a generation, then returning with a vengeance? I may not be much for snakes and grizzlies, or carrying a heavy backpack, but the tracking part is in my blood. Give me a room full of computers and cell phones and I'll find anyone you want, sometimes the most dangerous people on earth. Because here's the thing about the digital age: Everyone leaves a trail.

Some of them shouldn't be followed.

WWW.TRACKERSINTERFACE.COM
PASSWORD: STROGNOFE993

A 3:15 Original Story — Episode 201

LOUISIANA SWAMP MONSTER

A 3:15 Original Story — Episode 202

SNAP

A 3:15 Original Story — Episode 203

THE TUNNEL

A 3:15 Original Story — Episode 204

INTRUDER ALERT

A 3:15 Original Story — Episode 205

CORN MAZE

A 3:15 Original Story — Episode 206

OLD JOE BUSH

A 3:15 Original Story — Episode 207

THE CRUSHER

A 3:15 Original Story — Episode 208

ATTACK OF THE 40 FOOT CHICKEN